NORBY DOWN TO EARTH

Two red spots flared on Merlina's cheekbones and her lips trembled. "Wicked robot, I do have one thing my father found, something he tried out on you, at the lowest setting. Do you recognize this?" From her tunic pocket she took a tubular object with a switch on one side.

"That's a gun," said Norby . . .

ABOUT THE AUTHORS

JANET ASIMOV is the author of *Mind Transfer*, *The Second Experiment*, and *The Last Immortal* as well as many short stories and articles. ISAAC ASIMOV has written more than four hundred books, including the bestselling *The Robots of Dawn* and *Foundation*. He is the creator of the famous "Laws of Robotics." Janet and Isaac Asimov have been married since 1973 and have collaborated on the acclaimed "Norby" series.

PRAISE FOR THE "NORBY" ADVENTURES

"A charming set of characters . . . unique adventures."
—*School Library Journal*

"As usual, the Asimovs have crowded history, science, and a good yarn into a few short pages." —*Kirkus Reviews*

"Robotic fans and those who enjoyed Norby's earlier adventures will find this fast-paced plot equally diverting . . . funny!"
—*Booklist*

JANET AND ISAAC ASIMOV

NORBY DOWN TO EARTH

ACE BOOKS, NEW YORK

This Ace book contains the complete text of the original
hardcover edition. It has been completely reset in a typeface
designed for easy reading, and was printed from new film.

NORBY DOWN TO EARTH

An Ace Book/published by arrangement with
Walker and Company

PRINTING HISTORY
Walker and Company edition published 1989
Published simultaneously in Canada by Thomas Allen & Son
Ace edition/November 1991

ISBN: 0-441-58607-4

Ace Books are published by The Berkley Publishing Group,
200 Madison Avenue, New York, New York 10016.
The name "ACE" and the "A" logo
are trademarks belonging to Charter Communications, Inc.

PRINTED IN THE UNITED STATES OF AMERICA

10 9 8 7 6 5 4 3 2 1

To Planet Earth—
First and, so far, only home.
May we humans take better care of her.

CONTENTS

1

CRISIS AT HOME

Norby hovered on antigrav before his computer terminal and innocently blinked one pair of eyes at his owner.

"Jeff, do you mind if I do some research for my biography of MacGillicuddy? It's important."

"Go right ahead," Jefferson Wells said absently as he stared at his own computer terminal. "But do it as quietly as possible. I've promised myself that I'll use this interterm week for hard studying."

"Nobody's ever heard of the genius who put me together from Terran and alien robot parts," Norby said. "He should be memorialized. He should be posthumously famous. He should have a *statue*..."

"Sure," said Jeff.

"On Earth."

"Uh huh."

"In Central Park."

"Good idea. But I do need quiet..."

"And I have to do my research on Earth. Now."

"Norby, we're spending interterm week here in Space Academy and that's final." Jeff ran his fingers through his curly brown hair and wished he didn't have to grapple with space dynamics equations.

"I could jaunt over to Earth through hyperspace, do my research, and come back here before your next term starts." Norby's two-way hands clasped together over the silvery metal of his barrel body. Under the brim of his domed hat, his head sank further into the barrel so that only the tops of his eyes showed. He looked like a robot deserving pity and compassion.

"Why can't you do your research in the Space Command library? Admiral Yobo might give permission if you promise not to tie into the kitchen computer and ruin his meals. They mean a lot to the Admiral."

"I've already explored Space Command's library, without the Admiral's permission, and there's nothing about Mac."

"Space Command ties into all Federation libraries..."

"Not all. Ever since Manhattan tried to be the only independent nation within the Terran Federation, their data banks have been so jumbled that some of them are in a system all by themselves. Besides, I want to interview members of his family, those horrible people who sold me to that terrible used robot shop where you bought me."

"All right, Norby. I suppose you'd better go, but I thought I bought you as a teaching robot. Aren't you going to help me learn this ghastly space dynamics?"

"It wouldn't take you a whole week to study it if you'd let me mind-teach you, Jeff."

His owner groaned. "Oh no. The last time you taught me telepathically I didn't learn a thing for the test because you filled my head with one hundred and seventeen recipes for the worst kind of Space Command slumgullion—Norby, why are you interested in food when you can't eat?"

"All the recipes are slightly different in strange ways, so the mathematical permutations are interesting. I'm sorry I mixed you up, Jeff."

"I had to cram for the test at the last minute."

"But you passed. You always do when you try hard, even on your own. I'm proud of you, Jeff. You don't need a whole week to study. Come to Earth with me."

"No! Space dynamics is too hard!"

"Maybe you don't want to go to Earth to help me with my research because you're jealous of Mac, a poor old roboticist spacer who should have been honored..."

"For creating you?"

"I'm unique. I can't help it if I make a few little mistakes sometimes because the mix of alien and Terran robot parts doesn't always work perfectly," said Norby, who looked as though he would cry oily tears if Mac had made that possible. "But there isn't any other robot in the Federation with my abilities, and there never will be. I'm not appreciated."

"Norby, I do appreciate you, and you know it. I guess the Academy computers can help me learn space dynamics. Only you can be my friend."

"Thanks, Jeff. I'll learn all the space dynamics and try teaching it to you before I go to Earth—maybe tomorrow."

Jeff went on studying. It was quiet now in his Space Academy room that contained only a bunk, closet, desk, chair, and two computer terminals. On the pale green walls were two holopictures. One was of Jeff's parents, who had been killed in a space accident five years before, when he was ten. The devilishly handsome face smiling out of the other holopicture belonged to Jeff's twenty-five-year-old brother, Farley Gordon Wells, called "Fargo" after a remote ancestor who had acquired a bank's gold, a sheriff's daughter, and a coat of tar and feathers while passing through North Dakota.

"Terrible, terrible," muttered Norby, deleting a sentence.

"What is?" asked Jeff, before he had time to consider the consequences of starting another conversation.

"Selling a robot of my talents. Of course, if I'd known at the time I had so many talents I'd have escaped before the robot shop owner put me in that stasis box."

"If you'd escaped, you wouldn't have been in the shop for me to buy."

"That's right, and it's a good thing you bought me, Jeff, because most humans would have taken me apart to find out how to make other robots like me, not realizing that I contain alien metal from a previous universe, metal so rare that when you and I found some we had to take it to the far future..."

"We've had great adventures, you and I," said Jeff dreamily, leaning back in his chair. "All over time and space, thanks to your unusual talents. But you'd better not write about your talents or our adventures if you want to stay *my* Norby. Fargo and Albany Jones and Admiral Yobo and I are the only Terrans who know, and we'll keep your secret."

"Then I'll just write that thanks to my marvelous example of miniantigrav and hyperdrive, the Terran Federation has been able to invent its own version—poorly, of course. Very poorly. They'll never have my time travel or telepathy."

"I think I'd better go back to studying, Norby."

"Cadet!" shouted a deep bass voice.

Jeff nearly fell off his chair in his haste to turn around to see who had come in, but the door was closed and there was no one else in the room.

"Cadet, look at me when I'm talking to you!"

There on the computer monitor, instead of
space dynamics equations, was the massive
bald black head of Boris Yobo, head of Space
Command.

"I'm on the private tie-line," said the admiral.
"It's the quickest way to reach you more or less
in person. I've just had a call from Leo Jones—
you remember Albany's father, the mayor of
Manhattan, U.S. sector of the Terran Federation?"

Jeff suppressed a smile. Important person-
ages from Mars, like Boris Yobo, always used
tones of condescension when talking about the
original home of humanity, Earth.

"I remember, sir."

"Now don't get excited, Jeff, but Leo says
you'd better come home at once. Fargo's had an
accident and there's some sort of crisis..."

"What happened?" cried Jeff. "Is he in danger? What..."

"Goodbye, Admiral," yelled Norby, grabbing
Jeff's hand. "We're on our way to Earth!"

"But I have a transporter ticket for each of
you..."

The admiral's face, and everything else, disappeared before Jeff had a chance to object to
Norby's quick decision.

Gray gloom enveloped them, and in spite of
all the times he'd been in hyperspace, Jeff's
stomach tightened up because he knew that
just outside Norby's personal protective field
was a field of nothingness lethal to biological
forms. Inside Norby's field he could breathe un-

til the oxygen ran out, and thanks to a dragon bite on the far-off planet of Jamya, Jeff could talk telepathically with Norby.

—You should have waited, Norby. We don't even know where Fargo is right now.

—I can tune in to Fargo, not as well as to you but I'll get us to him. Under emotional stress my emotive centers rev up my inner works and I can do wonders. I hope.

—Please don't get mixed up in time, Norby. I want to arrive where and when Fargo is *now*, not in the past when he was a child before I was born, or in the future.

—Don't worry Jeff, I'm efficient. My hyper-drive will get us to Earth faster than using the Mars Orbit transporter from Space Command. I'm using hyperspace to zero in on a point in normal space that will be in the exact time frame that we just left.

The unmarked grayness of hyperspace vanished, and they were in normal space, staring at the bleakest landscape Jeff had ever seen. Across a bare valley was a mountain range equally bare of vegetation, bombarded by a heavy lightning storm from a cloud cover so thick that it was hard to tell what time of day it was.

Norby's protective field was still on, but in spite of it Jeff felt remarkably hot. The lightning was brilliant, but no rain seemed to fall, and everywhere the colors were wrong.

"Oops!" said Norby. The landscape vanished and they were back in hyperspace.

—Norby, I thought you said you wouldn't time travel! That wasn't Earth the way it is now. There wasn't any life and it was very hot even inside your field.

—Sorry, Jeff, I was trying so hard not to time travel that I was a tiny bit careless about space.

—What space? Where were we?

—The planet Venus. I missed Earth by a little...

—A *little!*

—I'll try again, Jeff. It's hard being a robot with emotive centers. You know I hurried away from Space Academy because Fargo needs us, but this time I'll be accurate.

—You'd better be!

—Here we go, Jeff. "Home!"

Norby's last word was said out loud, just as Jeff landed so hard on a carpeted floor that for a moment the wind was knocked out of him.

Directly before Jeff's eyes was a huge pair of strange plastic boots connected by an electric cord to a wall socket.

The pair of legs encased in the boots belonged to Fargo.

2

DOWN TO EARTH

From the knees up, Fargo's legs looked all
right. His middle section seemed okay, too, especially since it was encircled by the shapely
arm of the most beautiful cop in Manhattan,
Albany Jones. The rest of Fargo appeared to be
intact, and he was staring down at his kid
brother with his usual quizzical expression.

"You might have knocked," said Fargo.

"Are you badly hurt? What happened?" Jeff
asked, in between gasps for breath. He was relieved to see that Fargo was not in a hospital
but in the living room of their apartment on
Fifth Avenue.

At that moment the kitchen door was flung
open and a tall, robust middle-aged man loped
toward Jeff.

"Ho, Jeff," said Leo Jones, his thick yellow
hair giving him the appearance of a benevolent
lion. "I didn't hear the doorbell but I guess you
have a key."

"I'm the key," said Norby, helping Jeff to his feet.

"Fargo," said Jeff, "Admiral Yobo said there's a crisis here."

"Not really, not really," boomed Leo. "Fargo seemed to believe that only you could tend him properly, since my daughter has to take his place at a special Federation meeting. Boris Yobo insisted on having her as a substitute. Didn't he tell you about Fargo?"

"I wasn't given the chance to hear explanations," said Jeff, scowling at Norby. "How badly are you hurt, Fargo?"

"The injury was profound, but not severe," said Fargo.

"Profound!"

"He means," said Albany, "that he's not badly hurt, just badly inconvenienced, and needs your help."

"Badly, brother," said Fargo. "Very."

Jeff wiped his forehead "What was it—a secret mission for Yobo? Do you need my help finishing it?"

"It wasn't exactly that," said Fargo, turning slightly pink under his rumpled black hair. "Nevertheless, there's wicked game afoot..."

"Afoot is the word for it indeed," said Albany, grinning at Jeff. "And by game, he means pigeons."

"Pigeons?" asked Jeff. "As in stool pigeons, or as in beautiful women?"

"Feathered," said Fargo morosely. "I suggest that we refrain from discussing the matter."

"Mayor Jones," said Jeff, partly through clenched teeth, "I want to know the whole story, and I'm sure I can count on you to tell it."

Leo Jones, like most Manhattan mayors, loved to talk. "Jeff, my boy, your elder but not wiser brother was in Central Park with my daughter, who ordinarily carries a stun gun and is most efficient at combatting crime but that day was dressed as a mere civilian, due to the activity they were indulging in."

"Activity? Indulging?"

This time Albany turned slightly pink. "It's deep winter here, Jeff. We were ice-skating in the outdoor rink."

"We were all ice-skating," said Leo, with a wink. "For once Albany and Fargo were well-chaperoned, not that it did any good. Then this taxi appeared with polarized windows so it was impossible to see who was inside."

"I thought air cabs aren't allowed within the boundaries of the park."

"Except when summoned in dire emergencies," said Albany, "passengers have to get off at the boundary and walk in."

"Yes," said Leo. "Anyway, this taxi appeared, swooped down on the skating rink, and shot two of the ice-cleaning robots. They stopped working until someone pushed their 'reset' buttons, and then they worked as usual. They're stupid little machines about Norby's size."

"But I'm just little, not stupid," said Norby. "What happened to the taxi?"

"The taxi started to go away and Fargo ran after it."

Jeff turned to his brother. "Nobody can catch a taxi!"

"This one," said Fargo with a yawn, "was so old it went slowly and had trouble elevating off the ground. I was sure I could catch it and find out who was inside."

"There have been several incidents of small machines being zapped by some idiot in a taxi," said Albany. "Since none of the machines were permanently damaged, the police haven't been called in, but this time the park rules were disobeyed. I memorized the taxi's license number, but when we found it hours later the park trip record had been deleted from its tiny computer brain."

"But how did you get hurt, Fargo? What did the taxi do?"

"Nothing. I simply tripped . . ."

"Over a fat pigeon," said Leo.

"The pigeon was not hurt," said Fargo coldly. "But I sprained both ankles—worse than breaking bones, which can be knitted electronically in a day or two. Bad sprains require electronic baths for at least a week, so here I sit in these blasted boots, getting around the apartment in my electric scooter. I refuse to appear in public in these things."

"And this is the crisis?" asked Jeff. "You only sprained your ankles, but I had to leave my studying at Space Academy in order to tend you because Albany can't?"

"If you need to study, Jeff," said Leo, "you should go back to the Academy. I'll keep your lonely brother company."

As Leo said this, Fargo touched Jeff's hand, making telepathic contact.

—Save me, Jeff. I like Leo, but he's a born politician and insists on entertaining me when I want to be alone to work on the Great Federation Novel I've always planned to write if only I had time. I have time now, and if you don't stay in the apartment, Leo will.

Jeff sighed and smiled at Mayor Jones. "I'll stay with my brother. I can study here, and Norby has research to do."

"May I use the data banks at Gracie Mansion?" asked Norby.

"Certainly, certainly. Come for lunch tomorrow. That is, Norby can go down to our cellar computer room while you and I eat, Jeff. I'll be there, unless we have another of these computer store burglaries that the city is investigating."

"I don't like people who shoot cleaning robots or steal computer parts," said Norby.

"Nobody will steal you, Norby," said Leo. "You're too sassy. Now Albany, my dear, you have to pack to join Boris."

"I suspect that Boris planted that pigeon in the park just so Albany would be with him instead of me," said Fargo.

Goodbyes were said all around, the one between Fargo and Albany taking a considerable amount of time, but finally the Joneses left.

"Ah, alone with my novel at last," said Fargo, "or I will be as soon as Norby unplugs my boots and helps me onto my electric scooter. Now when I'm back in my room, working, should I start with a terrifying chapter about burglars stealing little robots?"

"No," said Norby, rising on antigrav to deposit Fargo neatly on top of the scooter.

"You mean you're only on chapter one of this Great Federation Novel?" asked Jeff.

"A great writer has to begin somewhere," said Fargo. "Oh, and while you're studying, Norby ought to zip over to Jamya to get Oola. A creative artist needs the comfort of something furry to pet, even if she's green."

Their all-purpose pet was visiting her mother on the planet Jamya, and since Admiral Yobo's one experimental hyperdrive ship had been wrecked, only Norby could go back and forth to the planet of the Mentor robots who had made the alien part of his machinery.

"She's not due back for a week," said Jeff. "Mentor First might be annoyed. Norby will go get her at the right time, which will be after I've finished studying."

"By that time my ankles will be healed and Albany will be back," said Fargo.

"I'll go to Jamya in a couple of days, Fargo," said Norby. "I want to talk to Mentor First anyway, for the biography. If Mentor First hadn't sent my alien self out to find that missing rescue ship sent from the Others, I wouldn't have been wrecked on that asteroid for Mac to find and fix. Mentor First and Mac are both like fathers to me."

"Norby's writing a biography of Mac-Gillicuddy," Jeff said to Fargo. "Except it sounds as if it's more about Norby."

"That figures," said Fargo, turning on his electric scooter and whizzing into his room.

"Now Norby," Jeff said firmly, "I am going to the kitchen to make a sandwich. I am going to eat it. Then I'm going to my room to *study*. I do not wish to be disturbed. Tomorrow we will have lunch with Mayor Jones and you can do your research."

"Okay, Jeff."

The peanut butter sandwich was delicious and Jeff was washing it down with apple juice when Norby came into the kitchen.

"Jeff, that taxi had some of its memory circuits wiped out. What if I run into the wicked person who would damage a robot mind like that?"

"Your memory is too complicated to lose," said Jeff, silently adding *I hope*. "If you're damaged in any way we'll hyperjump to Jamya so Mentor First can repair you. In the meantime, until the police catch the man who's shooting small robots, we'll be careful."

"I'm sorry I wanted to come to Earth to look up the data on Mac. I wish we'd stayed at the Space Academy, safely in orbit around Mars."

"We've been through many much more dangerous situations, Norby. As long as we're here in Manhattan, you'll do research and write, and

I'll study. It won't be exciting, but we'll manage just being down to earth this time."

"Down to earth," said Norby slowly. "Somehow that sends chills over my circuits."

3

GRACIE MANSION

Norby and Jeff walked up the steps of the broad lower porch of Gracie Mansion, Jeff's face chapped from the fast flight his robot had made from the Wells apartment.

"Maybe next time we'll take a taxi," said Jeff. "I've forgotten how cold winter gets, yet I'm not sorry the city's perennial fiscal crisis prevents it from building a dome."

"We won't take taxis," said Norby. "Taxis are dangerous, especially if someone persuaded a taxi to break the rules, go into the park, and let him shoot helpless robots. You should be grateful that you have my antigrav and propulsion system to get you where you want to go."

The mayor was late, due to a council meeting running overtime, so Norby went down to the basement computer room, chuckling metallically over the note the mayor had left for him. It read: "If you bollix my computer I'll have you

17

taken apart and I'll use your barrel to store jelly beans."

Jeff sat in the main hall, admiring the faux-marble floor, the curving staircase, and the fireplace with its painted wooden mantel and fluted columns. Through the windows he could see the frozen gardens, now terraced all the way down the slope to that saltwater tidal estuary known as the East River. Upriver was Hell Gate, the most turbulent part, with a name actually derived from the Dutch *hellesgarten*, meaning "beautiful passage." As Jeff tried to imagine what Manhattan had been like when the Dutch first came, he noticed that the sky was becoming a heavy slate color. It was going to snow.

While Jeff waited, a public tour ended. People put on their winter coats and went back out into the cold, but their tour guide stayed behind and smiled at Jeff. She was a smartly dressed middle-aged woman with an excellent figure, silver strands in her black hair, and a pleasant face that seemed vaguely familiar.

"Hello," she said. "Don't I know you?"

"I'm Jefferson Wells." Jeff thought that perhaps she'd been one of his early schoolteachers. "I'm called Jeff."

"I remember. You're the boy who helped us fight off the terrorists who were trying to take over Central Park some time ago. I believe they were after the entire Federation, too, but the misuse of our park was outrageous. I work at the American Museum of Natural History. I take people on birdwatching tours in Central

Park, and I'm also a volunteer guide here at
Gracie Mansion. My name is Hedy Higgins."

"Oh! Of course! Miss Higgins!" Jeff floun-
dered, because he'd remembered her as being
much older and plainer.

"I wear heavy tweeds and boots in Central
Park, but that doesn't mean they're the only
clothes I have," said Miss Higgins with a smile
at his discomfiture. Then she glanced at the
closed door to the mayor's study and her smile
vanished.

"When the tour went through the dining
room I noticed that the table was set for lunch.
I rather hurried the tour through so we
wouldn't disturb him."

"He's not back yet. I'm supposed to have
lunch with him. His daughter is engaged to my
brother. Do you know Mayor Jones? He's a
great guy."

"Yes, indeed. I mean, he has that reputation.
I have never met him, for all the times I've
taken tours through the mansion, and I think
I'd better leave before he arrives."

"Too late," said Jeff, looking out the window
and seeing Leo Jones bounding up the stairs.
"Here's the mayor—Miss Higgins, don't leave!"

She was headed for the back door when the
front one burst open and Leo Jones shouted,
"Hi, Jeff."

"Oh, dear," said Hedy Higgins.

Leo stopped short, his eyes wide. "By all
that's coincidental! I was just thinking of you
today, Hedy."

"Were you, Leo?" she said in a quavering voice.

"It was a difficult council meeting, what with the robot-zapper and the computer burglar and the way we keep finding more ancient water pipes when they freeze and burst. But I persuaded the council to allocate more funds for spring planting in Central Park's Ramble section. Plants that birds enjoy. For you, Hedy."

"Me?"

"I've kept track. I know you've become chief ornithologist at the museum, and I know how dedicated you are to Central Park. I never had the time—or the courage—to take a bird walk."

"Courage, Leo?"

"It's been such a long time. I always felt rotten for forgetting you after we left high school and went to different colleges. Then in grad school I married Albany's mother—dead now, poor soul—and then I became mayor, and very busy . . ."

"So busy you haven't noticed that a Hedy Higgins is a tour guide at Gracie Mansion, where by law all the mayors must live," said Hedy, laughing. "Leo, you haven't changed. Still a busy go-getter working twenty-four hours a day."

"Not today. Having lunch with Jeff here. Please stay and join us. I'd be honored, and from the pleased look on Jeff's face I don't think he minds."

• • •

The gracefully proportioned dining room had a fireplace, and Miss Higgins said the Duncan Phyfe sideboard bore 1800 willowware. Permiplastic protected the 1830 wallpaper that still showed blue sky over sylvan landscapes and Parisian monuments. Jeff ate a good lunch, watching with amusement as Leo entertained his high school sweetheart.

Was it possible that Hedy Higgins, the feisty, umbrella-wielding birdwatcher of Central Park, had become a Gracie Mansion tour guide so that she might meet Leo Jones again? Looking at her happy face, Jeff thought it possible. At fifteen it's hard to imagine that middle-aged people can fall in love, but as he watched Leo and Hedy, he decided it was happening.

All went well until over dessert the mayor began to talk about the mysterious person who rode in old taxis and shot small robots with some kind of electronic gun that didn't do any permanent damage.

"Funny thing," said Leo, "but it seems to be the same old taxi each time, and always with its trip records deleted by the time we find it. We've let it stay in circulation in the hope that some day we'll pick it up with the villain inside. We have to stop him, because other people could get the idea it's fun to zap robots, and maybe do real damage."

Jeff saw that Miss Higgins was not finishing her pie.

"If anybody had a gun that did damage robot

brains," Leo continued, "they could destroy our civilization. Why, if they knocked out the big computers, we'd lose touch with the rest of the occupied solar system. I've read about the computer riots of a century ago. They were bad, but fortunately human beings came to their senses and decided they'd rather retrain themselves for other jobs than go backward into the time when people were restricted to living only on planet Earth. You can't live anyplace else without good computer technology."

"I think I'd better leave," Hedy began softly.

"Nonsense. Stay awhile," said Leo. "Have you folks at the museum had any computer parts stolen by our other problem, the burglar?"

"I don't know. I really must leave," said Hedy, rising. "So good of you to invite me to lunch, Mayor Jones. And good to see you again, Jefferson Wells." She marched out so fast that the surprised mayor's jaw dropped open.

"But—wait, Hedy!" He got up, tripped on the rug, fell, picked himself up, and ran into the hall with Jeff behind him. The front door slammed and, through the window, they saw Hedy run through falling snow and get into a taxi that hovered over the icy lawn. It looked like an old taxi.

"I think I saw her use a cab-calling device that she took from her purse," said Jeff. "She wanted to get away fast."

"From me," said Leo mournfully. "Doesn't like me. Annoyed because I let too many years go by. Too late for us."

At that moment Norby came out of the hallway leading from the cellar staircase. "Had a good lunch, Jeff, Mayor?"

"It was delicious, and interesting," said Jeff cautiously.

"I had an interesting time, too," said Norby. "I found a data bank just for Manhattan residents and discovered that Mac's real first name was Moses. His wife died when his daughter was young, so Merlina inherited everything, including me. She's the one that sold me. I'll never forgive her."

"She's still alive?"

"Her husband's dead, but she isn't, and her two children live with her. She used to be an actress named Merlina Mynn."

"What!" Leo was astonished for the second time that day. "I was in love with Merlina Mynn!"

"Another love?" asked Jeff, beginning to feel cynical about the passions of Mayor Jones.

"I was eight, and I saw Merlina Mynn on Broadway. It was a long time ago."

"Well," said Norby, "Mac's daughter Merlina married a banker named Hilary Higgins, from the wealthy family that built Higgins House— the funny stone one with gargoyles that we've seen on Central Park West, Jeff. Merlina lives there with her son Horace and her daughter Hedy."

Norby blinked at the sudden silence. "Have I said something wrong? Is there any reason why I shouldn't interview these people?"

"Go right ahead, Norby," said Leo hoarsely. "Find out why Hedy never told me she was a Higgins from Higgins House, and who her mother was. When we dated in high school she was living with an old aunt and wouldn't tell me anything about her parents. Perhaps she didn't get along with them then."

"I'll ask her," said Norby confidently. "They owe it to me to tell me everything they know about Merlina's father, my Moses Mac-Gillicuddy."

"And Norby," said Leo, "tell her I've always thought Higgins House is a great old landmark and that I'd be delighted if she showed it to me. I'd ask her myself except that I'm a little nervous ..."

"And the phone number is unlisted," said Norby. "Jeff, maybe you'd better come with me when I pay a call. I'd like to try tomorrow morning."

"Okay, Norby, but we'd better go home now, because it's snowing heavily."

"Amazing, Jeff," said Leo. "To think that your robot was built by Hedy Higgins's grandfather!"

Jeff wondered why he suddenly felt that it was not so much amazing as ominous.

4

Higgins House

Next morning after breakfast, Jeff turned on his computer and was starting to call up the textbook problems on space dynamics when Norby stopped him.

"You promised to go with me to Higgins House, Jeff."

"After I've studied for an hour. At this rate I'll never learn space dynamics . . ." Jeff gasped as he stared at the screen. "But I understand this! How is it possible?"

"Because you have an efficient teaching robot," said Norby. "While you slept I did some mind-teaching. You should know and understand all the equations, and then some."

"Then some is right! If I tell the Federation *all* the equations you've taught me, Space Command will be kilometers ahead in improving their hyperdrive engines. But I won't tell them. Admiral Yobo won't like it."

"Why not? He might give me a medal."

"In the first place, he disapproves of cadets who can't master something by themselves, and I feel guilty because it's more or less by chance that your telepathic teaching worked right this time, and I should have studied it myself..."

"But you did, Jeff. You studied and studied and all I had to do was jog your mind a little. Didn't Louis Pasteur say that chance favors the prepared mind?"

"And in the second place, Admiral Yobo told me privately that he's changed his mind about forging ahead with hyperdrive. He thinks humanity had better go slow in getting out of our solar system because we're all so stupid and greedy."

"Well," said Norby, "even if you revealed those equations, nobody would believe you until they took years and years to check it a million times. Now please, let's go to see Mac's daughter."

Facing Central Park, Higgins House squatted on its corner like a refugee from another age—as indeed it was. The steep metal roof, punctured by several chimneys, curved over gables and odd bulges in the walls, which were three stories high. All the windows were covered by curlicued iron bars outside, and inside by heavy drapes. As Jeff looked up through the still-falling snow, he thought he saw one of the drapes twitch.

The largest gargoyle on Higgins House hung from the roof directly over the front door stoop with one eyelid closed in a wink, icicles hanging from its beaky nose, and its tongue sticking out at visitors. The cold seeped past the thermal lining of Jeff's boots. He was glad Norby had carried him over the deep snow that blanketed Manhattan and was not plowed away because the only vehicles that used the streets now were horse-drawn carriages or sleighs in winter.

The stone stoop in front of Higgins House had been shoveled just enough for one person to stand and reach the old-fashioned doorbell next to the large wrought-iron door. Norby hovered next to Jeff on antigrav and muttered metallically to himself as Jeff rang the doorbell.

A faint ringing somewhere in the house was the only result, for no one opened the door. Jeff rang again and looked up once more, just in time to get a shot of antifreeze-flavored water in his face.

"That gargoyle spit at me!"

"Maybe we'd better go home, Jeff, and write a letter."

Jeff turned to go, but at that moment a skier shot across Central Park West and up to Higgins House.

"Yo, Jeff! Norby!" Mayor Leo Jones, resplendent in a thermal bodysuit that demonstrated he was still a fine figure of a man, removed his skis and joined Jeff on the stoop.

"I phoned you, but Fargo said you'd already left so I hastened over from Gracie Mansion. This is Saturday—of course, I have my beeper in case the city government can't function without me—so I thought I'd join your visit to Higgins House. Say, is your brother all right?"

"He has sprained ankles."

"I mean in the head. He babbled about alien monster spies being in season this year."

"He's writing a novel and—there! I saw the drape move again. There's somebody watching us, and you'd better stand back, Mayor. When they don't want visitors they make that gargoyle spit at them."

"It is not patriotic to spit at the mayor of Manhattan," said Leo virtuously. He kicked the metal door with his ski boots. "Open up! This is your mayor speaking!"

The front door clanked and squeaked as it opened only a crack. There was a thick chain across the crack, and in the darkness beyond, Jeff thought he saw the dim shape of a human head.

"There are two of you, and a robot," said a rusty voice.

"I am Mayor Leo Jones, and this is Jeff Wells and his robot Norby, made by Moses MacGillicuddy. We wish to interview the Higgins family." Leo gulped. "And see Hedy, if possible."

The door slammed shut, there was the sound of metal scraping on metal, and the door reopened, minus the chain. In the dark vaulted hall stood a tall man wearing a patched tunic and a scowl. His bedraggled white hair had occasional black streaks, and old-fashioned eyeglasses were perched on his beaky nose. He had a strong resemblance to the gargoyle.

"The floor's stone," he said. "Wet won't hurt it."

Leo marched inside, deposited his skis against the unlit fireplace, and opened his bodysuit. Jeff and Norby followed rather uncertainly.

When the door swung shut with a clang, it was too dim to see much until a feeble light next to the door came on. Jeff saw that over the fireplace was the bas-relief of a dragon.

Norby clutched his hand to establish telepathic contact.

—That looks exactly like a Jamyn dragon, Jeff!

—MacGillicuddy must have taken it from the shipwreck when he found you. After Mentor First sent you through hyperspace to find the ship, did you have time to explore it before it crashed in our solar system?

—I don't know what was in the ship or what Mac could have taken from it. He never showed me that dragon sculpture.

"My name is Horace," said the man.

"Please inform the Higgins family that we are here," said Leo in the same tones he used when speaking to the robot butlers that some people could afford.

"I'm family. Horace Higgins. Grandfather made that robot. I remember mother talking about it."

"Did he make that dragon sculpture?" asked

Jeff, wondering if Mac had told his daughter about the shipwreck.

"Dunno. Maybe. He put something in the biggest gargoyle so we could scare away people we didn't want to see. Grandfather MacGillicuddy did lots of things. Wish I'd known him, but I was only ten when he died, and Hedy was a baby. I didn't know my father much either, but he and Grandfather Higgins were bankers and didn't invent anything."

Jeff realized that although Horace Higgins had the wicked features of the gargoyle, his eyes were those of a young and slightly bewildered child. "What do you do, Mr. Higgins?"

"I'm the janitor," Horace said proudly. "For Higgins House and the building we own next door. Mother won't let us keep robots, so Hedy and I take care of everything. She's over at the other house fixing the laundry room. Be back soon."

"We'll wait," said Leo. "In the living room?"

But Horace gestured to a bench along the wall across from the fireplace, so Jeff and Leo sat down. Norby rose on antigrav to inspect the dragon sculpture, while Horace gaped at him.

Now Jeff's eyes were adapted to the gloom, and he could see that there were closed doors further along in the walls. In the far end of the hall was a stone staircase that rose to a landing, divided in two, and curved up out of sight.

One of the doors opened and Hedy came into the hall.

"Leo!" She glanced back at the staircase and

then said, "I suppose I should have expected you to come. But you shouldn't have brought Jeff and his robot. You must take them away at once."

"Aw, let them stay, Hedy," said Horace. "I want to see all the things the robot can do."

"Miss Higgins, I want to talk to your mother," said Norby. "You and your brother are too young to remember your grandfather, but surely Merlina Mynn can tell me ..."

"Tell you what?" said another voice—a magical, husky voice that seemed to come from nowhere.

Suddenly the staircase was flooded with bright light that shone on what seemed to be a large oil painting hanging over the landing. It was the portrait of an exceptionally beautiful dark-haired woman in a white evening gown. She had huge, blue-purple eyes, perfect features, and an expression of such radiant kindness that you wanted to stay with her forever.

"Merlina Mynn!" said Leo reverently.

Someone was coming down the stairs, slowly, holding onto the bannister. She came into the light and turned, the portrait directly above her.

"Please go at once, Jeff," Hedy whispered.

"I may be old," said the woman, "but there's nothing wrong with my hearing. I don't think they should go until I make sure. I must know—are you really the robot my father made?"

She was tall and only slightly bent. Her eyes were still beautiful, and the bones of her face were still perfect. But the woman staring down at Norby seemed like a cruel caricature of the one in the portrait. Her white hair was drawn back from a withered face that looked as if she had been angry and self-pitying for much too long.

"Moses MacGillicuddy made me," said Norby. "I am writing a biography of him and I want to interview you..."

"No. You will write no biography of my father."

"Mrs. Higgins, please help me," said Norby. "I loved Mac, and I don't know why he never introduced me to you, or why you sold me without asking me where I wanted to go..."

"Silence, robot! Even if I wanted to, I couldn't tell you much about my father. He was always trying to invent things, or going on salvage trips, even after I let him have a laboratory here in Higgins House. He had my portrait painted and took that with him instead of me. He was more interested in making robots than in spending time with his own daughter. I hate robots!"

"Please, Mother," said Hedy. "It's not Norby's fault."

"Yes, it is. He was my father's favorite robot, and he must have stolen the legacy father left me."

"I didn't!" Norby yelled. "I wouldn't steal anything!"

"You did. I've never been able to find it."

"Mother, you've never told us what the legacy

was," said Hedy. "You just stayed on in Higgins House, searching and searching..."

"I'll tell you now. Father was taken ill suddenly, and on his deathbed he could hardly speak, but I remember his few words. He mumbled something and then said clearly, 'Keep the legacy safe... valuable... truth.'"

"That's all he said?" asked Horace.

"He died then. The lawyers didn't know what he meant."

"Perhaps he meant the dragon sculpture," said Norby, pointing to it.

"That silly dragon is not my legacy!" screamed Merlina. "Did he tell you it was?"

"No, he didn't tell me anything," said Norby, "but that dragon sculpture is alien art. I've scanned it and there's nothing inside, but it's good art. It's probably your legacy. Nothing else here could be."

—Except you, Norby.

—Except me. If I'm the legacy, please don't tell her, Jeff. I want to stay with you, not her.

"Robot, you must be lying," Merlina said. "I think you destroyed what my father left to me because you wanted him to yourself. You robots took my father away from me when he was alive, and you kept his true legacy from me."

"That's not true," said Norby, waving his arms. "It was you who left Mac! He said you weren't interested in him, only in your acting and in marrying a wealthy man."

Two red spots flared on Merlina's cheekbones and her lips trembled. "Wicked robot, I do have one thing my father found, something he tried out on you, at the lowest setting. Do you recognize this?" From her tunic pocket she took a tubular object with a switch on one side.

"That's a gun," said Norby. "So it was you who shot all the robots!"

"Yes. And my father used it on you, too, only you don't remember. He once told me he had a device that seemed to erase robot memory. I think he was sorry he'd tried it out on you, because he never found out afterward where certain parts of you came from. But I think he should have destroyed you because you are a bad robot, disobeying the prime rule of robotics that you must not harm any human being. You have harmed me in many ways, most of all by telling me what my father thought about me. I think you are dangerous, and that your memory should be wiped out."

"Wait!" shouted Jeff, trying to get between Norby and the gun Merlina was pointing.

She fired immediately, and Norby fell. His head, arms, and legs withdrew into his barrel and Jeff picked it up.

"Norby!"

There was no answer.

5

Tin Lizzie

Jeff held Norby tightly, trying to make telepathic contact, but there was no response. "You haven't just wiped out memory! You've used the strong setting and you've killed my robot!"

"Good," said Merlina faintly. Then she sagged against the bannister, the gun drooping in her hand. Leo plucked it from her fingers as Hedy ran to her mother.

"Let Horace take me upstairs, Hedy," said Merlina. "It's all over. I don't need the gun anymore. They can have it."

Jeff was so distraught that he didn't care what he said. "Merlina Mynn, you're the one who's wicked. Your father tried to tell you that your legacy was valuable and had something to do with truth. Well, the most valuable thing he owned was Norby, and it's Norby who finally told you the truth about yourself. *He* was your legacy, and you've destroyed him."

Merlina stared at him as if she couldn't understand. Finally she shook her head. "Doesn't matter. Nothing matters now. Go away. Never come back." Leaning on Horace, she walked slowly upstairs.

"I'm so sorry about your robot, Jeff," said Hedy.

Tears filled Jeff's eyes. "I will never forgive her."

Leo cleared his throat and patted Jeff on the back. "I'll call for a taxi to take you home, since Norby can't."

"Wait," said Hedy. "I've sent for Lizzie, Mother's favorite taxi—but I guess Mother won't be going out anymore."

When Leo and Jeff went outside holding Norby, there was a beat-up old yellow taxi hovering, its windshield wipers creakingly trying to cope with the snow.

"There's a rack for your skis on top, admirable human sir," said Lizzie. "Where to?"

"Leo," said Hedy, who was shivering in the doorway. "I feel so terrible about what happened. Couldn't you stay awhile?"

"If you don't mind, Jeff."

"I don't mind," said Jeff, who felt numb inside. He got into the cab, holding Norby on his lap, and told the taxi the number of his building across the park on Fifth Avenue.

"Wait," said Leo, rushing to the taxi. "Here's the gun, Jeff. I think you'd better take it to Space Command."

"Okay. Goodbye, Leo. And Hedy."

The taxi window rolled up and Lizzie elevated, rocking a little in the process because she was so old.

"What's in your shiny barrel, human sir?" said Lizzie.

"A dead robot. My best friend."

"Can't robots be repaired?"

"This one was special. There's nobody who could repair him..." Jeff stopped. If only he could reach Mentor First! But how? His own telepathy worked with physical contact, except that occasionally he and Norby tuned into each other by long distance telepathy. How could he do this with Mentor First? And if he did, was the Mentor's hyperdrive ship in working order?

Jeff thought about that strange alien race called the Others, who lived many times longer than human beings, who had created the Mentor robots to take care of the planet Jamya, and who had sent a supply ship to them. That was the supply ship that Mac had found wrecked, which had contained the alien Norby.

Mac must have salvaged from the ship not only Norby but the dragon sculpture and the alien gun. But why had the Others sent such a dangerous gun, a gun that could kill robots, to the Mentor *robots?*

Jeff and Norby had once found a present-day ship of the Others and had made friends with one that Jeff called "Rembrandt."

"If I can't mind-contact Mentor First, I've got to tune into Rembrandt. Maybe he can help undo the work of the gun."

"Did you say something, kind human sir?"

"Just talking to myself, Lizzie."

"You must be careful with that gun, sir."

"How do you know it's a gun? It doesn't look like one."

"I have seen it before. Mrs. Higgins used it so I wouldn't be able to tell the police anything about her and the trips she took with me."

"The trips to shoot robots?"

"As I told you, kind human sir, I no longer have access to the memories of those trips. I like Mrs. Higgins's children, but I do not approve of her. She is nasty to robots, but her father told me always to be nice to her."

"Her *father*?"

"Moses MacGillicuddy. He repaired me once, and after that I was always slightly different from the rest of the taxis. I seemed to be—*somebody*—I mean, I had—I don't know."

"You had a personality."

"A certain amount of character was built into Manhattan taxis a century ago when robot ground cabs were first used. People wanted taxis that sounded like humans who could tell jokes and discuss the weather and give news about the best tourist attractions. I was one of those taxis, and later I was remodeled as an aircab. My 'character' was merely programmed into my small brain, but after MacGillicuddy repaired me I seemed to have feelings and an identity."

"Did you discover any special talents?"

"Oh, no, human sir. MacGillicuddy told me I

would always be just a taxi, but that I would enjoy things more, and I do."

"Lizzie, did it hurt when Mrs. Higgins used the gun on you?"

"No, human sir. We have arrived at your destination."

"How will I call you when I want to ride in you again?"

A small taxi-calling disk slid out of the slot in Jeff's armrest. He put it in his pocket and got out of the taxi with Norby. "My name is Jeff Wells, Lizzie. I'll be calling you."

"I am sorry your robot friend is dead, Jeff Wells sir."

"So am I, Lizzie."

With tears on his cheeks, Jeff carried Norby into the building.

"There must be something that can be done to repair Norby, Jeff," said Fargo, much later.

"What? I've tried for hours to make telepathic contact with Mentor First or Rembrandt and I sense absolutely nothing."

"I've called Yobo. He's going to have them work faster on the Federation's replacement hyperdrive ship. You and I and Yobo will go to Jamya..."

"How? Do you know the coordinates? Only Norby did."

"Er, you're right," admitted Fargo. "I guess we've relied too much on always having Norby around. Are you certain he's dead?"

"Of course I'm not certain! And I won't let

myself be certain. I'm going to keep on hoping
I can save him somehow, because as long as I
hope, I'll keep trying, and maybe I'll stumble
across a way of doing it."

"I don't see any way unless you can reach
Mentor First or Rembrandt. With Mac-
Gillicuddy gone, there aren't any roboticists in
the Federation capable of repairing Norby, not
with all that Jamyn equipment and superalien
metal from the previous universe."

"We must try to reach Mentor First and Rembrandt by linking minds and putting all our
energies into long distance telepathy." Jeff
reached across the few pages of Fargo's manu-
script that were already printed out and
grabbed his brother's hand.

"I have never succeeded at long distance telepathy," said Fargo, "and with my ankles
bathed by electronic vibrations, we may have
interference."

"We'll try with your boots turned on and then
turned off."

They tried. Over and over.

Nothing worked.

Just before he went to bed that night, Jeff
received a hycom call from Admiral Yobo.

"I heard about your problem, Jeff. I'll sure
miss that impudent little robot. He got us into
a lot of scrapes, but he usually got us out of
them again. I want to reassure you that we're
going ahead with the new hyperdrive ship as

fast as possible. Although it won't be ready for months..."

"We don't know Jamya's coordinates, Admiral," said Jeff wearily. "Didn't Fargo explain?"

"Yes, in his second call. He's more worried about *you* than he's letting you know. Somehow we'll find a way to get to Jamya and Mentor First. Perhaps our new ship's computer can find the coordinates in the Hopeful's computer..."

"Fargo's scout ship is in for an overhaul..."

"Ye gods, I'll have to make sure they don't wipe out everything in the computer..."

"They probably have. I don't think we can count on the Hopeful, although Norby did use it many times. But we don't know how he transferred his own hyperdrive to the Hopeful's computer."

"Why do you think it's taken the Federation so long to make a hyperdrive ship? From Norby we knew it was possible, but we couldn't learn how to make one from him. We had to invent our own, and with great difficulty."

"Admiral, are you saying that your new ship is running into problems?"

"Yes, but don't despair, cadet. We'll find a way to Jamya if we have to circumnavigate the universe."

Jeff thanked Yobo but went to bed very much in despair. He kept looking at Norby's closed-up barrel in the corner, and he couldn't sleep. The noises in the overworked heating system were not helping, so finally he got out of bed

again and went into the living room. The blinds
were up and he saw that it had finally stopped
snowing.

Moonlight shone on Central Park, tracing
out the white decoration of snow on each dark
tree branch and old stone wall. A few lights
still glimmered in the buildings over on Central
Park West, but Manhattan seemed quietly
asleep. Jeff knew the city was always awake,
especially further downtown, but right now he
felt as if he were the only one looking out on
the beauty of the park. The only one sad with
loss.

An aircab with one burnt-out headlight flew
slowly up Fifth Avenue, turned, and came
slowly down again. It paused near Jeff's window and blinked the remaining headlight.

Jeff opened the window. "Lizzie?"

She came closer. "I did not mean to disturb
you, Jeff Wells sir. I had no calls tonight and I
thought I would hover near your apartment in
case you needed me in a hurry."

It was bitterly cold, but the sharp clarity of
the unpolluted air seemed to clear Jeff's mind.

"I'm going to rescue Norby," he told Lizzie.
"I haven't figured out how, but I will."

"I'll help if I can."

"Thanks, Lizzie. You're a good taxi and
friend."

"I am honored, Jeff Wells sir, but you'll get
too cold with that window open. If you're going
to sleep now I will go downtown in search of a
fare."

"Okay, Lizzie." He watched her make her rather lurching way through the air over Fifth Avenue, heading south, and then he closed the window and got into bed.

To help himself go to sleep he tried to recite a version of his solstice meditation, but it wouldn't come. The anguish over losing Norby seemed about to overwhelm him again when he suddenly felt that eerie sensation deep inside that always told him an idea was percolating.

"But what?" he asked himself.

He took a deep breath, made his facial muscles curve into a cheerful smile, let the breath out, and let his muscles all relax.

"I am a child of the universe," he whispered. "Norby is still part of the universe, no matter how damaged he is. There is a way to help him, and the way is somewhere in my mind, only I can't find it at the moment."

Jeff sat up and really smiled this time. He looked over at the chair where Norby's closed-up barrel rested, and he said: "Norby, I don't think you can hear me, but sometime today I heard something that will help. I don't remember what it was, but perhaps it will come up out of my memory if I don't get in its way."

Jeff lay back, pulled the covers up, and closed his eyes.

"Something I heard..." he was half asleep. "Lizzie?"

He finally slept.

6

Some Medicine

The next day Jeff felt blank, as if the mysterious idea had disappeared for good. The more he forced himself to remember, the blanker he felt, so he decided to stop straining for it. He would do something else and let the idea come up of its own accord. He went back to studying, although the thought of finishing his training as a Space Cadet and going on to work in Space Command as he'd planned seemed dull and tiresome if he couldn't have Norby with him.

Another day passed, the end of interterm week was much closer, and still Jeff had not been able to help Norby.

Leo Jones called that evening to ask Fargo about Jeff and Norby and to report that although his friendship with Hedy Higgins was developing rapidly, she'd told him that it would be better for her mother if nobody visited Higgins House. Merlina Mynn had sunk into a severe depression, moaning that now she would never have her legacy.

"She'll never have Norby, damaged or undamaged," said Jeff. "I bought him and he's mine. And I love him even if he's just a barrel of dead parts."

"Sure, Jeff," said Fargo soothingly. "But I wish you'd stop studying for a while and go for a moonlit ride in Lizzie. She hovers around our windows so much that our neighbors complain she spoils the view." On his electric scooter he went back to his own room and to his novel, which he said was not coming along well at all.

Jeff hailed Lizzie and was about to climb in from the living room window when he heard Fargo yell.

"Hey! What do you think you're doing!"

There was a tremendous crash and the sound of Fargo swearing loudly. Jeff ran and burst into Fargo's room in time to see the overturned scooter next to two grappling figures, one wearing dark clothes and a ski mask, the other in redstriped pajamas and electronic boots.

With one of his more exotic judo maneuvers and helped by the weight of the boots, Fargo pinned his adversary to the carpet and tore off the ski mask.

"Well, well," said Fargo, panting a little, "this looks like an actor too old to play Dracula but still trying. Is it anyone we know?"

"He's Hedy's brother Horace Higgins," said Jeff. "What are you doing here, Horace, and how did you get in?"

Horace sat up, rubbing his neck. "I'm good with locks. I can get into most places that are locked up, except I think I picked the wrong room this time."

"But what did you come here for?"

"That old robot—the one Mother shot. I thought I could use the parts inside the body. I looked you up in the phone book and thought if I removed Norby's machinery while you were asleep you wouldn't know and you could keep the barrel around for sentiment."

"What were you going to do with Norby's insides?"

A sly look came over Horace's melancholy face. "I have a hobby. Mother doesn't know about it. Hedy says I mustn't let her know because she hates computers and robots."

By this time Fargo had righted the scooter and with powerful arm muscles had hauled himself and his boots onto his bed. "So you have a hobby, Horace? Playing with robots?"

Horace smiled happily. "Playing with computers. I have a workroom in the basement of our other house. There's a connecting door so Hedy and I can go through to take care of things. Mother doesn't know about my workroom. Hedy fixed it for me. She said Grandfather MacGillicuddy would have approved of my hobby."

"Tell me the truth," said Jeff. "Were you going to steal Norby's insides, or all of him?"

Horace hung his head. "I really wanted all of your robot. I hoped I could repair him. I have a lot of computer equipment in my workroom."

"And did you get it by stealing from computer stores? The Mayor told us that there's been a rash of computer burglaries lately," said Jeff.

"That was me. I mean, that was I. Are you going to tell the police?"

"Not if you promise never to do it again."

"Hedy tells me not to take things. When she catches me she sends money to pay for the equipment. It's just that it always seems to be late at night, after the stores have closed, when I need a part badly. I don't like going out in the daytime with so many people about. I like to be alone with my machines. I have some that play games with me. Do you think I could fix Norby and he'd play games?"

"I don't think so, Horace," said Jeff. "Now I'll take you home in Lizzie—I was just going out anyway."

"It's late."

"I need to think of some way to help my robot."

"If I can help, I will. Thank you for not calling the police." He stood up rather shakily and nodded to Fargo. "And I hope I didn't hurt you. I didn't realize you were handicapped."

"Just temporarily," said Fargo, magnanimously not mentioning the fact that even though he was wearing medical boots he was the equal of an elderly burglar.

Lizzie flew over the nearest transverse street, where taxis could legally cross Central Park, and Horace talked to Jeff about his hobby.

"I wish Mother had given that gun to me. I wouldn't have used it to wipe out robotic memory the way she did to poor Lizzie here. I might have been able to use the gun's energy for something else."

"What?" asked Jeff.

"I don't know. Most destructive things can be used for good if you know how. Do you think you could figure out how?"

"The gun can be used for good," said Lizzie suddenly.

"What?" asked Jeff, who had not taken Horace seriously.

"MacGillicuddy told me so, but he said it was still a very dangerous gun. That is why I warned you, Jeff Wells sir."

"But didn't he say anything else about the gun—how it could be used..."

"No, sir. Not to me. And it was a long time ago."

"Blast!" said Jeff. "How can I possibly find out how to use the gun the right way? Maybe it would restore Norby."

"Not if Norby's energy has been used up," said Lizzie.

"What do you mean?"

"After Mrs. Higgins used the gun the bad way on me, I sometimes was so weak from loss of energy that I couldn't antigrav very well and had trouble going back to the garage. I solved the problem by—but it's illegal. I'd better not tell anyone what I did."

"Lizzie!" Jeff shouted. "Stop. Turn around. Go back to my apartment. I'm going to get Norby and you're going to tell me what you did to get energy. Horace and I will keep your secret, won't we, Horace? Especially since what Mrs. Higgins did to you was also illegal."

"I never thought of that," said Lizzie. "I will go back."

Jeff was almost attacked by Fargo, who thought more burglars had shown up, but he was soon back in Lizzie with Norby on his lap. "Now show us, Lizzie."

She flew over the transverse street once more and sank lower and lower until she went right under the middle overpass, the only one in the entire park that was not a man-made bridge but tunneled right through solid rock. Huge icicles hung from the rock ceiling where water seeped down.

"I always wait here to see if anyone's around. It's late and this transverse doesn't go to Lincoln Center, where there are always lots of people, so I guess I'm safe."

Very slowly, she moved out of the tunnel and up, staying just over the trees. Jeff saw little Belvedere Castle behind them on the other side of the overpass, and ahead was the densely wooded Ramble section of the park. He knew it well, or thought he did, but when Lizzie sank to just above the ground, following a path that was almost too narrow for her, he lost his bearings and didn't know where they were.

The moonlight filtered through the trees only slightly, because the moon was no longer full, and the frozen snow on the trees cast big shadows. Lizzie's one headlight picked out the path, and finally Jeff saw something familiar, an old-fashioned lamppost beside a high stone arch.

Lizzie elevated until she was next to the lamp, and an oddly jointed arm telescoped out of her front end. The arm ended in two little arms that each had plierlike fingers with which she removed the outer casing of the lamp and then unscrewed the bulb. She put the bulb and the lamp casing into a pocket in her front end and gestured to her passengers.

"Jeff Wells sir, you will have to climb out on my hood and place your robot on it. I suggest that you put one of my rubber floor mats under Norby so you won't feel the electricity I'm going to channel to him."

"But it might hurt him!"

"He is already hurt," Horace said in a kindly way. "I will hand Norby to you after you are safely on Lizzie's hood."

Jeff climbed out and then took Norby and the rubber mat from Horace. "Lizzie, Norby has no plug or socket, but I've seen him take a charge of electricity through his sensor wire. It's inside his hat now, but perhaps if you touch his hat..."

"I will do so." She touched Norby's hat with one little arm and used the other to dig into the electric socket of the lamp. Jeff watched, shivering in spite of his thermal clothing.

"There," said Lizzie, withdrawing her arms. "I have transferred a great deal of electric energy to Norby, and I think some of mine—oh dear!"

Lizzie was falling. Fortunately, she didn't have far to go, but the small crash threw Jeff and Norby off her hood and into a snowdrift.

"Are you all right, Jeff?" Horace asked anxiously, sticking his scrawny neck out of the taxi window.

"I'm not hurt," said Jeff, struggling up out of the snow and looking for Norby, who must have gone way into the drift, under the frozen snow crust.

Horace opened the door with much difficulty because the snow was in the way. "Let me help."

"You don't even have boots. How did you get to our building from Higgins House?"

"I took another taxi when Lizzie didn't come. I didn't expect to go out into the snow."

Jeff found Norby and hauled him out. He was still closed up and silent. Sadly, Jeff brought Norby back inside Lizzie and closed the door.

"Didn't the electricity help?" asked Lizzie.

"I guess not," said Jeff. "Please Lizzie, and Horace—please be quiet while I concentrate. I'm going to try to reach Norby by—well, by mind contact. It's something we've learned to do. If there's any flicker of life I'll find it."

Jeff concentrated with his eyes shut, but he felt nothing.

"Jeff, I think you'd better . . ." Horace began.

"*Shhh!*"

And then, "Is that all you could do for me, Jeff—let a stupid taxi shoot bolts of electricity through my valuable body?"

"Norby! You're alive!"

7

GOING HOME

"I have never received worse treatment," said Norby, his half-head rising out of his barrel. His arms and legs emerged. He looked wonderful to Jeff.

When Lizzie spoke her voice was oddly tinny and soft. "I apologize, Norby, but it was the only way I knew to restore energy depleted by that awful gun."

Norby patted Lizzie's floor, where he was standing. "No apologies necessary, dear lady. The electricity was jolting but it certainly helped. The gun discharged all my energy and I couldn't move even to get into hyperspace to recharge."

"You recharge in hyperspace!" said Lizzie and Horace simultaneously.

"Don't tell anyone," said Jeff earnestly. "Please."

"What a marvelous robot," said Horace. "I am

so pleased that mother did not destroy it after
all."

"I'm cold and tired," said Jeff. "Lizzie, take
Horace home. Norby and I will ..."

"No, we don't, Jeff," said Norby. "I can't take
you. My special talents are gone. That's why I
didn't hear your attempts to reach me telepathically, which I assume you made. And I
can't hyperdrive or antigrav."

"Oh, Norby!"

"I'm just an ordinary robot now. Will you still
want me?"

"Of course, Norby. I love you, and I'm so
happy you're still going to be my friend."

"Lizzie will take us all home," said Horace.
"I'll pay—Hedy gave me some extra money this
week so I'd buy robot parts instead of stealing
them."

"Unfortunately, kind human sir, I cannot
perform my taxi functions at the moment. You
may have noticed that my heater has stopped,
as well as my clock. I need to recharge. Helping
Norby drained all my energy except for the little fusion pack that keeps my modest brain
going."

"Just plug yourself into the lamp, Lizzie,"
said Norby.

"Impossible. My arm won't reach that high
and I can't antigrav. You will have to send for
the repair service."

"I'll climb up the lamppost, plug myself in,
and reach down to your arm," said Norby.

"Perhaps none of you noticed," said Lizzie

faintly, "but there are no lights in the park. We've blown a fuse or something."

"I'll walk to the nearest phone," said Horace. "Where is it?"

"You can't walk without boots," said Jeff. "I'll go to the boathouse. There's a phone just outside it."

"I'll come with you, Jeff," said Norby.

"I'd have to carry you in this deep snow and I'd probably slip and fall. I'll go alone. You three wait here."

"Please hurry, Jeff Wells sir. If the repair truck does not come soon, my taxi engine will need such serious repairs that the garage will probably remove my robot brain and install it in a factory somewhere."

"I'll send the truck as soon as possible," said Jeff. Plunging out into the snow, he headed through the trees up a small hill and down again toward the boathouse.

Lizzie's calling disk had the number of her garage on it, and Jeff confidently punched it into the computer keypad of the phone booth next to the boathouse. Nothing happened, and he realized that the phone booth had not lit up when he entered.

He didn't have Fargo's vocabulary of expressions to be used when circumstances were at their most irritating, but he tried all the ones he knew as he slogged on to Fifth Avenue and his own building. The electricity was out there, too, so he had to walk all the way up to his apartment, and since the electronic doorkeeper could not function and recognize him, he hammered until Fargo woke up and let him in.

First he had to explain things to Fargo.

". . . and so even if Norby's missing his special talents, he's still alive, but I have to help Lizzie get recharged or Horace will freeze in the Ramble, or freeze walking home, and Lizzie's brain will probably be sold to a factory—and how can I get in touch with the garage when the phones are out?"

"Interesting," said Fargo. "A long time ago the phones were not connected to the city electrical system, so when the lights went out the phones didn't. I think that's still true of the phones of hospitals, police, fire department, and government—that would include the mayor, so just zip over to Gracie Mansion . . ."

"Do you have any idea how many blocks we are from Gracie Mansion? Unplowed blocks?"

"Call another taxi—oh, no phone. Wait—I've just remembered that I have an emergency battery charger somewhere. It was in the Hopeful but I took it out when I put the ship in for overhaul. A battery charger might give Lizzie enough oomph to make it to her garage. Try the hall closet."

"You're a genius, Fargo!" Jeff said a minute later.

"I endeavor to give satisfaction," said Fargo smugly. "At least Albany says so. Now take a flashlight in case the blackout continues and our best extension cord in case it doesn't. Be careful—not that you're likely to be mugged at

this hour and temperature. Given my indis-
position, it's good that you're young and can
use vigorous exercise."

"I feel older and tireder by the minute," said
Jeff, repackaging himself in his winter clothes.

"It's not much past your bedtime. You'll still
get some sleep if you can charge up Lizzie so
you won't have to carry Norby out of the park,
to say nothing of Horace. Good luck."

The walk back seemed longer and colder and
more frightening because the bulky battery
charger made slipping more likely and his
flashlight seemed to be showing paths he'd
never seen before. He saw Bow Bridge ahead
and knew he'd taken the wrong turn. He shut
off his flashlight to see by moonlight, but the
sky was filled with clouds. Then he saw a light
moving back and forth in the trees and headed
for it.

"Hi, Jeff," said Norby. "I found a flashlight
in Lizzie's trunk and thought I'd signal to you.
Your light went the wrong way so I had to wade
through the snow. I miss my antigrav."

"I know, Norby," said Jeff, picking him up.
"I miss it too, but not nearly as much as I missed
you."

In spite of Lizzie having no heat, Horace
wasn't frozen because there'd been a blanket in
the trunk, too. Lizzie herself was not doing well.

"My motor's almost dead, Jeff Wells sir. Did
you get the garage on the phone?"

"The phones are out along with the electricity, but maybe this battery charger will work enough for you to get back to the garage for a better recharge."

"Thank you, Jeff Wells sir. Actually, I'm afraid of my garage. I think they'll find out that I've been taking electricity from the lamppost and they'll confine me to quarters. They've been threatening to scrap me for some time now. Could you possibly buy me?"

"I wish I could, Lizzie, but Fargo and I don't have the money. He can just barely manage to keep his scout ship. Can't the Higgins family buy you? What about it, Horace?"

"I want to, but unfortunately we have very little money, only what comes in from rents and from Hedy's salary."

Norby used the battery charger on Lizzie until it was exhausted. Her motor coughed into action, but her antigrav was too feeble to lift her from the snow.

"Maybe I can still get out of the park on my own," said Lizzie. "It's a good thing that antigrav vehicles are still made with wheels, just in case. Get inside, everybody."

At that moment all the park lamps lit up, and Jeff got out of the taxi with the extension cord. Norby held one end to Lizzie, and Jeff climbed up the lamppost with the other end. He felt as if the cold metal of the post was freezing his fingers right through his thermal gloves.

But it worked. After another recharge, Lizzie elevated easily on antigrav.

"Lizzie," said Horace, "we must take Norby and Jeff home first because Jeff has walked twice through the park and must be tired and cold."

"I will do so at once," said Lizzie.

Not only was it snowing again but the windowsills of the Wells apartment were judged dangerously icy, so Lizzie parked on the roof right in front of the stairwell door, which responded to Jeff's voice and opened.

"Goodbye, Horace and Lizzie," said Jeff. "Thanks so much for helping me restore Norby."

Horace opened Lizzie and went inside the roof door to shake hands with Norby. "I'm sorry my mother took away some of your powers, Norby. Grandfather MacGillicuddy was not a very good father to her. She was always unhappy, and now that she's old she's not very normal. Neither am I, but I'm happy and I love robots."

"Mac loved his daughter," said Norby. "I know he did."

"But she doesn't," said Horace sadly. "I hope we will meet again. It has been an adventurous night for me. And I promise not to burgle..."

"Hey!" shouted Jeff, staring past Horace through the falling snow. "Something big's coming—Horace, look out!"

Jeff grabbed Horace and pulled him further into the stairwell just as something huge dropped on the roof, crushing Lizzie beneath it.

8

Visitor

The building stopped shaking and so did Jeff. "Are you all right, Horace?"

"I'm not hurt—but Lizzie is. I guess the storm made another ship pick your roof as a landing space, only they didn't see Lizzie. She must be dead."

"I am not dead, Mr. Higgins sir, but my body is ruined. I will be unable to take you home. Please tell the ship that dropped on me to remove itself so the garage can pick up my remains in the morning. I fear that now my brain will end up in a factory for sure."

"I can't see well through the snow," said Norby, "but there don't seem to be any markings on that ship and..."

The ship's airlock suddenly opened, and silhouetted against the light from the interior was a dark figure over two and a half meters tall. It stepped forward, and as it loomed over him Jeff saw that it had two sets of arms, three eye patches, and many old dents and scratches in its metal body.

"Mentor First!" Jeff shouted.

"Father!" said Norby.

"That's an awfully big robot," said Horace, shrinking against the wall of the landing. "Is it something experimental from Space Command?"

"I know Admiral Boris Yobo well," said Mentor First in only slightly accented Terran Basic.

"Oh," said Horace. "Well, I guess that's all right then, but did you have to crash onto my favorite taxi?"

"I came out of hyperspace on the coordinates Norby once gave me for your home, Jeff. I did not expect such weather, or that there would be something else on your roof, because when Norby brought Oola to Jamya, he told me the Hopeful was being overhauled." Mentor First said all this in the Jamyn language. He added in Terran Basic, "I am so sorry, sir, that I have damaged your vehicle."

As snow accumulated inside the stairwell, Horace shivered and said, "You should be! Maybe I ought to call the police anyway. Space Command can't do this to innocent taxis..."

"Horace," said Jeff, "you'd better spend the night on our convertible couch. It'll be hard getting another taxi." In Jamyn he added, "And besides, we don't want anyone to see what's on our roof."

"But patrol cars will spot the Jamyn ship in the morning," said Norby in Jamyn. "I think

Fargo still has a can of white paint from that time he redid the bookcase. Mentor First and I will paint the Hopeful's call letters on the Jamyn ship and maybe nobody will pay attention."

"They'll still see the remains of Lizzie," said Jeff.

"Are you speaking in a special Space Command code?" asked Horace, still shivering but obviously enthralled.

"Sort of," said Jeff. "Mentor First, can you lift your ship off Lizzie a little, put her inside it, and then lower your ship—very gently—to the roof?"

"I am strong. It will be no problem."

"What are you going to do with my brain?" asked Lizzie. "Even if my chassis is a hopeless wreck, my shielded brain with its fusion mini-motor is still valuable, and the salvage crew will expect..."

"Lizzie," said Norby, "my father and I will take good care of your brain. I think your garage had better adjust to the fact that one of its oldest taxis is simply missing. Maybe they'll think your antigrav gave out when you were over the Hudson River, down in the part that's over that deep underwater canyon. I suppose Jeff, being the way he is, will try to find a way of paying the garage, but in the meantime, please trust me and my father. We will be careful. And now, Jeff, take Horace downstairs before you both turn to icicles."

Mentor First went back into his ship and returned with a ball of green fur that he placed in Jeff's arms. The ball unwound itself, yawned, and licked Jeff's chin.

"Thanks, Mentor First," said Jeff. "Fargo's writing a novel and will be glad to have Oola for comfort."

"Oola's mother is having another baby and Oola is jealous," said Mentor First. "I thought Norby should come for her early, but when I tried to reach Norby telepathically, I felt nothing. That had never happened before. I was worried that something had gone wrong, and since my ship would have been detected instantly if I'd gone to Space Command, I decided to try you and Fargo. You didn't respond telepathically without Norby's help, but I sensed that you were here in your Manhattan home. I hope I have not damaged it . . ."

"Just bend over when you and Norby come downstairs after you've taken care of Lizzie. The doorways aren't high enough for a Mentor robot."

Horace was so exhausted that he went right to sleep in the living room, but tired as he was, Jeff sat up in Fargo's room telling him what had happened.

Cuddling Oola, Fargo pointed to the small chunk of plaster that had fallen from his ceiling. "Good thing Admiral Yobo had our roof reinforced when he allowed me to park the Hopeful up there. And I'm glad the Hopeful was in for overhaul because Mentor First might have landed on her, too. After all, this is his first trip to Earth and the weather in Manhattan would unsettle anyone."

"But what's going to happen to Lizzie—we have to pay damages, and they'll take her brain to a factory..."

"Jeff, you make a career of worrying. Now there are still a few hours to daylight, which fortunately comes late in the dead of winter, so as your older brother, guardian, and substitute parent, I insist that you go to bed and sleep."

Jeff did.

By morning the snow had changed to freezing rain, icing the park trees and the rest of snow-covered Manhattan. While Horace and the Wells brothers ate breakfast, Mentor First gazed out of the window as the rain slowly petered out and feeble sunlight filtered through the cloud layers.

"Where's Norby?" asked Fargo.

"He is trying to reassure Lizzie that she'll be all right," said Mentor First. "While you slept, Norby and I put the remains of her body into my ship. Then we attached her brain to the ship's computer. I will take her with me to my, ah, headquarters. She seems pleased at the idea."

"Good," said Fargo. "What do you think of our city?"

"There are so many castles here."

"Those are just tall buildings we call skyscrapers," said Fargo. "Some buildings used as living quarters are also very high, but ours is only medium-sized because it's so old."

"This snow, as you call it, is a remarkable phenomenon. Do you have much of it on planet Earth?"

"Only in the colder parts. Manhattan is a cold part, in the winter. Earth tilts, you know, so we have seasons top and bottom. We're hot in summer."

"It sounds as if robots like you are used to living inside the domed colonies we have in the rest of the solar system," said Horace. "Is this your first time on Earth?"

"Yes," said Mentor First. "And I am indeed used to a very pleasant, equable climate. I have never seen snow or all this icing before. I can hear trees crack in the park. How do you stand living here? Don't you want a regulated climate?"

"Certainly not," said Fargo. "The natural climate of our Manhattan is invigorating, making us enjoy and appreciate the adaptability of the human body as well as the creations of the human mind."

Jeff laughed. "Fargo, I've noticed that you like to stay inside when it's too cold or too hot."

"Pay no attention to my kid brother," said Fargo, spearing another hot biscuit. "And don't you think Horace should phone his sister to let her know he's all right?"

Guiltily, Horace swallowed the last of his peaches and yogurt and stood up. "I have imposed too long on your hospitality. Much as I would like to stay and talk to this marvelous robot, I must go home and make sure the heating system is working properly in this cold. Our tenants object if they don't get enough heat . . ."

The doorbell rang.

"At this hour of the morning?" asked Fargo.

"It's almost noon," said Jeff. "We all overslept." He opened the door and Leo Jones strode in.

"Hedy says Horace has been out all night and she doesn't know where he is—Horace! What are you doing here?"

The door opened again and Norby walked in, astonishing Leo. "Norby! You're alive!"

"It's a long story, Leo," said Fargo. "Suitably edited, I will regale you with it over another biscuit while Jeff and Horace put on their coats."

In his own room, Jeff asked Norby how Lizzie was.

"She's okay, Jeff. Since she has access to the data bank of Father's ship, she knows where he comes from and is willing to go there, the first Manhattan taxi ever to visit Jamya, except that she isn't a taxi anymore. She's a little sad about it."

"I wish she were still a taxi. I've called for a cab but either the companies put me on hold or they say I'll have to wait hours."

"Father can carry Horace home."

"Sure, and be arrested . . . wait, Norby, that's a good idea. Go get that big piece of cardboard that came with that poster I bought."

When Jeff and Norby joined the others again,

they carried a placard that urged: Buy Cob's Industrial Robots. A heavy string loop was attached to the top of the placard.

"If you wear this, Mentor First, nobody will think you are unusual," said Jeff. "Especially if you wear my extra ski helmet over your top eye patch and hide your other set of arms under a cape..."

"Not my red satin lined evening cape," said Fargo. "Don't you think some industrial robots could have four arms?"

"Okay," said Jeff. "Mentor First will carry Horace home. If he doesn't mind carrying me and Norby, too, we might be able to show him the dragon sculpture over Horace's mantelpiece. And Mayor Jones, would you mind very much calling Hedy and telling her that we're on our way?"

"I'll call, and then I'll join you. The robot can pull me on my skis if I have trouble on the icy snow."

"I hope my mother doesn't see Mentor First," said Horace. "A robot that big will make her wish she could still destroy robots."

9

Made by the Others

Higgins House looked even more fantastic with ice on all its peaks and curves and outcroppings. Mentor First looked up at it as he deposited Jeff and Horace on the front stoop.

"Now this must be a castle," he said.

"Perhaps you're right," said Jeff. "If every human's home is his castle, then Higgins House certainly qualifies." He was about to warn Mentor First about the spitting gargoyle until he saw that ice completely enveloped the gargoyle's head.

Hedy welcomed them inside, saying nothing about the odd appearance of the big robot or the placard he was wearing. Jeff suspected that Mayor Jones knew more about the Wells family's adventures than he let on and had sworn Hedy to secrecy.

Norby, still held in Mentor First's lower arms, showed no desire to get down. "Where's your mother, Miss Higgins?"

"Upstairs. She doesn't leave her room anymore. She's suddenly become a very old woman, and she weeps all the time. She can't bear to go downstairs because she has to pass the portrait of herself when she was young and beautiful. She keeps saying that she'll just die never having her father's legacy because she killed his robot. If I told her she did not kill him . . ."

"Please don't tell her anything," said Jeff. "Norby's special abilities have been destroyed, and we don't want to explain all that, and if she sees Norby she will remember he revealed that perhaps Mac felt shut out by her self-centeredness, too."

"Yes," said Hedy. "I understand."

Mentor First was staring at the dragon over the fireplace.

"Leo, have you had lunch?" asked Hedy.

"No. Didn't get more than a bite of Jeff and Horace's brunch over at the Wellses'."

"Then let's go to the kitchen and we'll lunch together. The museum is closed today, and I think Horace can show Higgins House to Norby and Jeff and Mentor First."

"I'll go down to my workroom and clean it up a little. I'd like Norby and Mentor First to see it," said Horace.

When they had gone, Mentor First said in Jamyn, "Jeff, that dragon sculpture was made by the Others. MacGillicuddy must have found it in the wrecked ship, along with Norby."

"When I first saw it," said Norby, "I didn't think it had any moving parts or electronic insides. I can't tell anymore because my scanning talent is gone. Do you agree?"

"Yes. It is only a work of art, but it is a very good one. It belongs in Jamya."

"Don't say that," said Norby. "Merlina Mynn has had everything taken away from her. We have to leave the dragon."

"I will leave it," said Mentor First. "But I sense that there is more in this house that comes from the Others..."

Horace came back, beaming. "Please come see where I work. Nobody's seen it but Hedy until now."

It was a large basement room in the other building, filled with such odds and ends of equipment that Jeff couldn't see how Horace did anything in it except look for things. Horace, however, seemed to know exactly where everything was and showed them his chess-playing machine and his automatic water music fountain. Jeff didn't mention to him that his most prized "inventions" had been in common use for centuries, and he hoped that Mentor First would understand that Horace was a human being who did not have adult mentality.

"An interesting assortment," Mentor First said, picking up an old wooden object with many beads strung on wires.

"That's an abacus," said Horace eagerly. "You can do arithmetic on it, but I'm not much good. The pocket computer is so much easier. I even have the instructions for the abacus. Would you like to have it as my gift?"

"Thank you," said Mentor First gravely. "The, ah, children who live where I come from will much enjoy this. And what are these?"

Horace looked at the small flat objects in Mentor First's lower left palm. "Transistors. Really old ones, but they probably still work. I've also got some microchip boards."

"I do not understand," said Mentor First.

"In the history of Terran robotics," Norby said, "these devices made advanced computers possible and were used until the invention of the microbubble computer brain."

"I thought I could use microchips to run my electric trains, but the trains are so old that ancient transformers work okay. See?" Horace removed a large canvas cover from a corner table. On the table was a miniature landscape of hills and villages and a tiny railroad with signal crossings, tunnels, bridges that went up and down, and a station. Horace touched a switch and the train chugged along the track, sending out miniature puffs of what looked like smoke.

"That's wonderful!" said Jeff, fascinated. He'd had a model space station when he was younger, but he'd seen model trains only in museums.

"It's easy to make an old-fashioned transformer," said Horace, pointing to the box-shaped one that he used for his model trains. "Even I can do it. I have an extra, Mentor First. Take it and the transistors. You can compare the way each amplifies current, although of

course the transistors do many other things
that are difficult for me to understand."

"Thank you," said Mentor First gravely, as
if he were being given precious jewels. He took
the spare transformer from Horace's bony
hand. "I would like to inspect these things. I
may even be able to use them for the drago—I
mean, the children's toys. Thank you very
much."

Jeff looked longingly at the model railroad.
"That's a great train, Horace. You've made it
look and run so well."

"You can come over any time, Jeff," said Horace. "We can play with the train and you can
tell me what it's like in space. I'll never go
there."

"Perhaps you will."

"No. I don't like to go out of the house, and
I hate to leave Manhattan Island. I'm staying
here."

"Jeff!" Leo was yelling from the connecting
basement door between the two buildings. "We
have to go."

"Yes," said Mentor First. "There is someone
near who is poisoned with hatred. I can sense
it."

"I don't want to see Merlina Mynn again,"
said Norby.

Hedy joined Leo and they both came into the
workshop. "My mother saw you all come in the
front door. She didn't notice Norby because
Mentor First was carrying him closed up, but
she is upset because she doesn't want any robots

in the house. I told her that I had sent for a repair robot to look at the heating system. You'd better leave from this building instead of going back into Higgins House. She doesn't mind if Leo stays awhile."

When the two robots and Jeff were outside and safely across the street in Central Park, Mentor First looked back at Higgins House.

"I wish I could examine that house again. There is something alien to Earth there. Something powerful."

"The dragon sculpture?" asked Jeff.

"I wouldn't have thought so, but perhaps I am wrong."

"Is it evil?" asked Norby. "It's hard for me to believe that anything the Others tried to send to Jamya could be evil, but the gun certainly is."

"Evil?" said Mentor First. "This is a human concept, perhaps, but I can understand it. I do not know. I sense only dimly, because this is not my planet nor the biological species I understand, but it seems to me that there are bad thoughts and something else that does not fight them but waits for change."

"What could that be?" asked Jeff.

"I do not know." Mentor First straightened the sales placard hanging down his back, lifted Jeff into his arms next to Norby, and marched through the snow of Central Park.

• • •

Fargo, Jeff, Norby, and Mentor First talked and talked for the rest of the day, reviewing and rereviewing the problem.

"I have examined Norby," said Mentor First. "I cannot tell what is wrong. It seems that his major talents have been wiped out, and I do not know how to make new parts for him that would restore the ability to hyperdrive and move on antigrav. I am afraid to take Norby apart."

"I'll trust you, Father. You made me."

"Only part of you, Norby. I inserted the miniantigrav components, as well as the mechanism to permit your travel in hyperspace, but after MacGillicuddy found you, he mixed them up with many other things, all intricately tied together in such a fashion that only he could safely take them apart."

"And he's dead," said Jeff. "I had a faint hope that his grandson would be able to help, but poor Horace is a simple man with simple intelligence, not a robotics genius."

"How about letting Yobo's scientists help you with the problem, Mentor First?" asked Fargo.

The Mentor tickled Oola's stomach with one of his huge hands and said, "Can you trust the admiral's scientists?"

"No," said Norby. "They'd lose interest in helping me and would want to take you apart, Father."

"Norby's probably right," said Jeff. "We'll have to think of something else."

"Say, Jeff, you haven't even shown Mentor First that gun yet." Fargo's eyes narrowed as he looked at his brother. "I thought you told me Lizzie told you Mac told her the gun could be used for good. Did you follow that?"

Jeff smiled faintly. "She also said Mac told her the gun was very dangerous."

"Go get it, Jeff," said Fargo.

Jeff went to his room, unlocked the desk drawer where he'd put the gun, and took it out, looking carefully at it for the first time since that awful night when he'd come home thinking Norby was dead.

The gun was a stubby cylinder of pale orange metal that felt almost like warm satin to the touch. If you moved aside a guard plate, you could put your thumb into a deep depression and push forward one notch, or two. Merlina must have pushed two notches when she shot Norby.

One end of the gun was of the same orange metal, rounded off and closed. The other was open, and when Jeff looked inside he could see a translucent gold layer of something that didn't seem to be metal, a layer that glowed faintly.

The more he held the gun, the more Jeff didn't want to let it go. It seemed almost alive, a mysterious alien device that somehow made you feel powerful just holding it. He didn't want to bring it to the other room.

Suddenly he felt as if he had been holding that gun for many years, that it was his and he could never get rid of it; yet he felt too that he would never be able to use it because it might destroy him.

Jeff squared his shoulders and walked into the living room. Fargo, Norby, and Mentor First turned to stare at him.

"What's wrong, Jeff?" asked Norby.

Jeff held the gun out to Mentor First. "Please take this device. It does funny things to people who hold it. No wonder Merlina Mynn is so disturbed. I don't know how Mac managed."

"He used it on me right after he found my Jamyn self," said Norby. "The memory of what exactly happened is gone, as well as the memories of Mentor First constructing me, but I now can remember Mac holding the gun. After he made me from the Jamyn robot and a Terran robot, he said he'd never alter my memory again. That was the last I saw of the gun."

"Maybe the gun scared Mac and he hid it," said Fargo.

"He must have used the first setting," said Mentor First, still staring at the gun but making no gesture to take it from Jeff. "The first removes robot memory patterns. The second must remove robot talents, as well as energy. Used long enough, the second setting could probably destroy a robot brain if only by depleting all the energy."

"Please take it," said Jeff. "See if there's some way it can be used to give back Norby's talents. If not, take the gun to Jamya, where it was supposed to go."

Mentor First touched the gun and drew back as if burned. "I don't want to use this device. It is dangerous to robots. It should be used by biological beings."

"You mean if a robot holds it and activates it the gun might damage that robot?" asked Jeff.

"Perhaps."

"Then why did the Others send it to Jamya?" asked Fargo. "When the rescue ship was sent, the Mentor robots there were only beginning to civilize the Jamyn dragons."

"So it wasn't meant for the dragons to use as a way of controlling the Mentors," said Norby. "Perhaps the gun had instructions with it, meant for the Mentors. A way they could use it without harm, for some constructive purpose."

"That must be it," said Mentor First. "MacGillicuddy may have found the instructions, too, but since he didn't read Jamyn he probably threw them out."

"Not if he was anything like Horace," said Jeff. "He'd have kept them in his workshop in Higgins House. We'll have to show Horace a sample of Jamyn writing and ask him if he's found anything that looks like it."

"You probably won't find the instructions," said Fargo. "Horace might have made a toy out of them, or more likely his mother threw them out. After all, she had the gun, and if the instructions were with it..."

"Blast!" said Jeff.

"What could the constructive purpose have been?" asked Mentor First.

No one could answer, and Jeff locked the gun back into his desk drawer.

10

One Talent Left

Jeff slept badly that night. He kept dreaming that Merlina Mynn was chasing him, waving a flat Norby who looked as if he'd been squashed by Mentor First's ship. When he turned to pull Norby away from her, Merlina laughed hysterically and suddenly became as young and beautiful as she'd been when her portrait was painted.

Jeff woke up sweating and realized that the room actually was too hot. The heat was still on full blast but the weather had changed again. A warm front had moved in, and Jeff could hear dripping as the ice melted.

As he lay there, conscious of the fact that Norby and Mentor First were in the living room speaking softly in Jamyn, he remembered the night when he'd been certain that somewhere in his brain was useful knowledge that might help Norby—something he'd heard. He still couldn't remember it, but now he was sure that Lizzie had said it.

After breakfast, during which Fargo grumbled about the problems of plotting a novel, Jeff asked Mentor First to let him into the Jamyn ship so he could talk to Lizzie in her new incarnation.

Both robots went with him, and Lizzie was delighted.

"I am so glad you are here," she said. Her voice was more musical coming from the ship's computer, but it had the same Manhattan accent. "I'm lonely. The computer isn't much company for a robot taxi brain who's used to humans. I've told it all the jokes I know and it hasn't any sense of humor."

"Lizzie," said Jeff, "I'm trying to remember something you said about the gun. Could you repeat it?"

"I said that Moses MacGillicuddy told me the gun could be used for good, but that it was still very dangerous."

"He never said what kind of good?"

"No, but . . ." Lizzie paused, and Jeff couldn't help thinking it sounded odd for her Manhattan taxi voice to come from the control board of Mentor First's spaceship.

"But what?" asked Norby.

"Nothing definite. I had the impression—but robot brains are not supposed to be intuitive, so perhaps I should not talk about . . ."

"Lizzie!" yelled Norby. "Stop thinking like an ordinary Terran robot brain. You're not any-

more, and not just because you're attached to
Father's ship. You haven't been ordinary since
Mac changed you. You probably do have intu-
ition, just the way you have feelings. Tell us
what impression you had."

"Well, I thought that perhaps MacGillicuddy
was talking about the change in me as a good
thing the gun had done, but I have no evidence
for this. I do not know if the gun changed me."

"Perhaps it did," said Mentor First. "But
how? We don't know how to make the gun work
in a nondestructive way."

"If only we could reach the Others," said Jeff.
"Surely they would know."

"Perhaps it is just as well that the gun never
reached us," said Mentor First. "It might have
caused more harm than good. But you are right,
we could learn from the Others. Since all the
Mentor robots were activated by the main computer after the Others left Jamya, I have never
seen an Other, although I know that you and
Norby have."

"We've seen them in the past, the present,
and the future," said Norby. "We know one
Other well. We named him Rembrandt. He's
alive in our present, somewhere in the universe, either in normal space-time or in hyperspace."

"He'd help us if he could," said Jeff. "He's an
artist, so maybe he did the dragon sculpture."

"No, Jeff," said Norby. "As biological beings,
the Others live much longer than humans, but

the rescue supply ship must have been sent out
before Rembrandt was born."

"He still might know about it," said Jeff.
"And about the gun. Let's try, all of us, to concentrate on him. I know that Norby's telepathic
powers are gone, but the rest of us have some
and we can try."

"Do you mean me, too, Jeff Wells sir?"

"You, too, Lizzie, especially now that you're
part of Mentor First's powerful ship ... *ship!*"

"What's the matter, Jeff?" asked Norby.

"I keep forgetting that this very ship we're
in is the one that the long-ago Others sent as
a supply ship to Jamya. The ship that was
wrecked on an asteroid in our own solar system,
along with The Searcher—you as you were
when Mentor First made you, Norby."

"So what, Jeff? Maybe a human like you for-
gets things like that, but Mentor First and I
haven't forgotten it."

"But has this ship ever been thoroughly
searched? Maybe we could find something else
the Others sent, or instructions, anything that
might explain the working of the gun and what
the dragon sculpture means."

"This ship has been gone over many times
since Norby brought it to Jamya," said Mentor
First. "Since we didn't know about the gun or
the sculpture, we didn't look for instructions
that may be hidden somewhere. Let us look
now."

They searched every square millimeter of the
Jamya ship but found no instructions for any-

thing. There was one cabinet, however, that had marks on it as if the door had once been forced open. But there was nothing inside.

"I was going to use that cabinet for specimens, in case I ever went exploring for minerals on other planets," said Mentor First. "Somehow, I am always so busy on Jamya that this trip to your Earth is the first one I have made. I think this cabinet was empty when the ship came to us."

"But it's big enough for the dragon sculpture," said Jeff, "and that drawer would just hold the gun and instructions."

"Look," said Norby. "There are odd clamps on the inside of the cabinet door, top and bottom. And the shelves are recessed so that if the clamps were holding something, the door could still close."

"But what shape could it have been?" asked Mentor First.

"The clamps remind me of the things that hold plumbing pipes to a wall." Jeff closed the cabinet door almost all the way and looked in. "I think there'd be just enough room for a tubular object like a pipe to be held in the clamps."

"Only it isn't there now and we don't know what it could have been," said Norby.

"I don't know either," said Lizzie. "I have searched the memory banks of this rather idiotic computer my brain is attached to, and there's only the notation that the cabinet contained special art objects sent by the Others.

No list. That's not much help, is it?"

"It helps," said Norby. "It confirms Jeff's deduction."

"Wait," said Jeff. "If—and it's only an 'if'—the gun was actually in that drawer, then it would have fallen under the classification of 'art objects.' That means the gun is meant to be used for art in some way, not for destroying robot memory or talents."

"Yes, but how?" asked Norby. "Lizzie, can you find anything else that might explain how the gun should be used?"

"No, Norby, but I am now more closely linked to the power of this ship. I believe I can contribute more to your joint efforts to reach Rembrandt's ship telepathically."

"Let's try," said Jeff. He held Mentor First's lower right hand while the big robot touched the control disk of his ship's computer, linked to Lizzie. "Come on, Norby."

"I can't do it anymore."

"You can be part of the linkage anyway."

"Maybe I'll spoil things," said Norby softly, his head sinking into his barrel body until only the tops of his eyes showed. "Maybe I'm not just lacking talents. Maybe I'm damaged in some other way that will be dangerous if I'm linked to other minds."

"Norby, my son," said Mentor First, "do not despair. We will find a way to help you. Link with us. We are not afraid. Are we, Jeff?"

"No."

"Lizzie?"

"Oh no, kind Mentor sir. I'd never be afraid of Norby."

Jeff held out his other hand. "Come on, Norby."

Jeff held tightly to the two robots on either side of him. He was gazing directly at the view-screen above the ship's control board. There was Central Park, glittering in sunlight as the warmth melted the ice and snow. He could see tiny Belvedere Castle—he reminded himself that he ought to show Mentor First the only "castle" in Manhattan—and he thought that if only the Mentor could go into the huge bulk of the Metropolitan Museum to see genuine *human* art . . . he was not concentrating.

—I can show anyone the tourist attractions of Manhattan [said Lizzie telepathically]—I mean I could when I was a taxi . . .

—I will be glad to see human art someday [said Mentor First]—but now I think we should concentrate on the Others. You know what they look like, Jeff. Picture them in your mind.

Ashamed of the flightiness of his thoughts that Mentor First and Lizzie could now read, Jeff shut his eyes and tried again to concentrate.

He forgot about the view of Central Park and in his mind formed an image of the Other called Rembrandt. Tall, four-limbed and three-eyed like the Mentor robots they had created, the Others were still vaguely humanoid, with expressions of great calm and beauty on their strange faces.

Oh, how he wanted to see Rembrandt again!

Suddenly Jeff's stomach seemed to drop and he heard Lizzie scream out loud.

"I'm falling!"

Jeff opened his eyes as Mentor First broke the linkage, lunging at the control board to take control of the ship.

Then Jeff looked at the viewscreen and gasped, for the ship was falling onto scrubby trees in a landscape he had never seen before.

11

MAC

The ship stopped falling, but it had smashed several trees and was only a meter from the ground.

"Thank you, Mentor First," said Lizzie. "I should have turned on the antigrav myself, but I was so surprised to find the roof out from under the ship that I forgot. Having the capacity for emotion may be all right for a Manhattan taxi but it is not safe in a spaceship. No wonder your computer is so dull."

"Lizzie, since you're part of my computer now, please memorize the exact coordinates of the location my ship was in before we started falling."

"I do not need to memorize," said Lizzie, somewhat acerbically. "I retain the coordinates. Or your computer does. Or something. I'm a little confused, but the coordinates are available. Do you wish to return the ship to them on antigrav?"

"Yes."

The ship rose and then stopped. Jeff grunted and said, "If you don't mind, Mentor First, I'd like the ship to go twice as high."

"Very well. It is done."

From the new height, Jeff had a much better view. Now he could see that the land had thick forests with scattered outcroppings of rock and a few meadows. In the distance he could see the sheen of water and beyond it more land.

"Is the ship turned around?" Jeff asked.

"Yes," said Norby. "I'll have the sensors turn so we can see what's in every direction."

From the shadows of the trees, the sun seemed to be high overhead, so it was hard to tell which direction was which—and then Jeff saw the moss and lichen on the nearest big trees. Moss grew on the north sides of trees. The first view had been east, thought Jeff, watching as the viewscreen showed the view changing to the south, where the land seemed to be an unending wilderness. Then as the sensors turned toward the west, Jeff saw more water—a large river, and beyond it cliffs whose igneous columnar structure was unmistakable.

"Humans!" said Mentor First. "Where are we?"

People were moving among the trees, and one bronze-colored man leapt to the top of a high rock, shouting and waving his bow. He took an arrow from the quiver he carried, fitted it to his bowstring, and sent it thudding harmlessly against the side of the ship.

"Those are Manhattan Indians," said Jeff. "And that's the Hudson River, with the Palisades beyond. We've gone back in time, before 1626 when the Indians sold the island to the Dutch. Take the ship higher and you'll be able to see all the way south down to the tip and New York Bay."

"The view is spectacular," said Mentor First, "and I am sure you are proud of living on such a beautiful island whatever time you're in, but how did we get to your seventeenth century— or even older?"

"I think I did it," said Norby. "I was trying so hard to make myself have telepathy again that I forgot I hadn't tested my ability for time travel. I've tried antigrav and hyperdrive and I know they don't work, but time travel obviously does."

"Rembrandt does not exist in this time period," said Jeff. "Perhaps the Others who made the gun do exist now, but how can we find them? Shall we concentrate on telepathy again?"

They tried and tried, with and without Norby linked in, but nothing happened. Neither Jeff nor Mentor First felt any hint of mental contact with the Others.

After an hour, Jeff said, "Norby, if you got us here, can you take us home again?"

"I'm not sure, Jeff. Perhaps we'll have to go to Jamya to live the rest of our lives."

"We can't do that," said Jeff. "Mentor First is already on Jamya at this time. We can't go where one of us already exists. Try to get us to our own time just after we left it."

Mentor First said, "Lizzie, take the ship to the exact coordinates in space that we had when we were on Jeff's roof."

"Yes, sir."

Norby plugged into the ship by himself, closing both sets of eyes to concentrate on returning to the proper time. After five minutes he opened the back pair and looked at Jeff.

"I wish I could talk to Mac."

"You can't go back to a time and place where you exist."

"Okay, I know. I just wish..."

There was a lurch, and suddenly the roof of Jeff's building appeared below and civilized Manhattan all around them.

"Something's wrong," said Jeff. "The tall apartment house that was built on Central Park West last year isn't there."

The ship's sensors were picking up more voices, and this time everyone could understand the language because it was ordinary Terran Basic.

"Hey! You've got Space Command markings, so you don't belong on my roof! We were asleep and didn't see you arrive, but now that you're here, leave at once or I'll send for the cops. Manhattan is a private country and you outsiders have to go through channels to get entry clearance."

The sensors turned to show on the viewscreen a tanned middle-aged man dressed in bathing trunks. With him was a middle-aged woman holding a folded deck chair. She was in a bathing suit and a huge floppy hat. Both of them looked angry.

"This must be many years ago, before Manhattan decided to give up sovereignty and join the Federation," said Norby. "I wonder if I could find Mac. He was a young man then. Maybe he could help me. This is long before he bought a salvage ship and found me."

"The man on the roof has left shaking his fist," said Mentor First. "He is probably going to call the authorities. Lizzie, if Norby can't take us to our own time, please go someplace else."

"Where?" asked Lizzie. "This ship's too big to hide under the transverse tunnel in the park."

"Wait, wait," shouted Norby. "Go over Central Park, slowly. Maybe my sensors aren't completely out. I sense—Mac. I wanted to see him so much that I tuned into the only time when I could see him as an adult, before he found me. I must see him..."

"You can't, Norby," said Jeff. "You'll change your own history if you do, and everything that's ever happened to us. That's going to change me, and Mentor First—everything."

Norby paid no attention. "He's in the park. Lizzie..."

"I am taking the ship where Norby wants."

"Lizzie!" yelled Jeff. "You don't understand about time travel. You don't know how dangerous it is, because the future, which is our present, can be changed!"

But Mentor First's ship was hovering over Central Park, just skimming the treetops so that it would be less obvious to patrolling antigrav cars.

"He's in a rowboat on the boating pond," said Norby with great excitement. "Don't you recognize him, Lizzie?"

"Yes, Norby. That is our Moses MacGillicuddy when he was younger." She brought the ship down to the surface of the lake, right next to the rowboat.

MacGillicuddy smiled at the ship and yelled, "Hey, Space Command—aren't you lost or something?"

Mentor First grabbed Norby. "You must say nothing, Norby. You must not go out of the ship to see him."

"I know," said Norby. "I'm not totally stupid. I know the laws of robotics and I wouldn't do that much harm even if I wanted to very badly, as I do. What I want is for Jeff to lean out of the airlock, pretend to be asking for the best museums tourists can go to, and find out if Mac is married and whether or not he wants children."

"What's the point of that?" asked Jeff.

"I'm not sure," said Norby. "Even if I can't ask Mac to help me, I might be able to help Merlina later."

Jeff stood in the airlock and waved to MacGillicuddy. He rowed closer, his good-

natured face resembling that of his grand-
daughter Hedy, except that he was much
younger. It was a chilly spring day, the early
cherries only just in bloom, and the daffodils at
their peak. Mac wore a baggy sweater that
looked as if he'd had it for years and a green
silk scarf that looked brand new.

"You seem too young for Space Command,"
said Mac.

Jeff swallowed hard and tried to imagine how
Fargo would behave under these circumstances. Fargo would put on an act and make others
believe in it.

"I'm a Space Cadet," Jeff said, glad he didn't
have to lie about that. "I'm part of a survey
we're taking..."

"If you're interviewing Manhattanites about
the prospect of joining the Federation, I'm all
for it. It's silly for a small island to believe it
can go it alone in a solar system that's united.
The original idea was to make money from vi-
sas and whatnot, but it backfired, and now the
Feds are charging *us*. Tell your bosses that once
we join the Federation I'll be the best salvager
in the business. I've just bought a used spaceship and..."

"This is a different kind of survey, sir. It's
sort of a random sampling of people who don't
have nine-to-five jobs. This isn't a weekend, is
it?"

"Don't you know?"

"I just got in from, ah, far away..."

"Well, you're right. It's a Monday and I'm not

at work. I usually am, at a robotics company, but today I'm celebrating and doing some heavy thinking about all the things I want to accomplish, the inventions I want to achieve—you know, the future. Planning for it, and that sort of thing."

"What are you celebrating? A local holiday?"

Mac laughed. "Just my own. My wife had our first child yesterday, a baby girl we've named Merlina because she's so magically wonderful. I helped deliver her, and after I do my heavy thinking here on the lake, I'm going to see her again."

"Congratulations, sir. It sounds as if you're very happy to have a daughter."

"I'm delighted. It's just what I wanted. I'm going to see to it that Merlina has the best that life can offer. I'm going out in the solar system and find treasures for her, things that will give her happiness all her life."

"That's fine, sir. And now we have to go. It's so cold here in the park that there aren't many people. We'll finish our survey further downtown."

"But what *is* the survey? You never told me."

"It only applies to people who work for themselves."

"Come back in a year or two, because then I'll qualify."

"Good luck, mister."

"And to you, cadet."

The Jamyn ship lifted from the water's surface and went high enough to hide behind a cloud. Norby sat at the controls, determined to take the ship to their own time.

"I can't concentrate," Norby said. "I keep thinking about Mac and Merlina. He loved her very much."

"Most new fathers love their babies," said Jeff.

"This was special. He did want the best for her. Maybe he overdid it, working in his ship, salvaging and inventing. It took so much time away from home that Merlina grew up resentful and self-centered, but Mac probably didn't notice. He loved her no matter what, and he meant well."

"Lots of people do," said Jeff. "We must go home."

"Yes," said Mentor First, going to join Norby at the controls. "You concentrate on our own time, Norby, and I will help you. We must return, for that is the only way we can find the Others who know you."

"Look in the viewscreen," said Lizzie. "Three patrol ships are approaching. They are blinking red lights. In the Manhattan of my day, that would mean I committed some traffic violation like excess speed and would get a ticket, but I have not been speeding."

"Stay where you are!" boomed an amplified voice picked up by the ship's sensors. "In spite of your unusual shape your call letters identify you as belonging to Space Command. You are not registered as passing through Alien Immigration. You have violated the air space of the sovereign nation of Manhattan and we will tow you into custody..."

"Quick!" yelled Jeff. "Go into hyperspace before they put force grapples on us!"

Mentor First moved quickly. The ship plunged into the cloud bank, away from the patrol, and then the misty cloud changed to the much eerier gray of hyperspace.

"Safe," said Mentor First.

"I don't like it here," wailed Lizzie. "If this is hyperspace it gives me the creeps all through my circuits! I am a Manhattan machine and I want to go back to my own space and time!"

"We all do, Lizzie," said Jeff. "Norby, did we move through time as well as into hyperspace?"

"I don't know. I was trying, but I'm not much good at anything these days."

"Jeff Wells sir."

"Yes, Lizzie?"

"I know this is Mentor First's ship, but he is a robot and I am programmed to think of humans as my masters. I must report first to you, kind human sir..."

"Report what?"

"I'm doing my best to get a reading from the sensors of this alien ship that I'm now part of, but apparently they don't work in hyperspace. Nevertheless, I can tell if anything touches the hull. I am reporting that something has attached itself to the airlock of this ship, sir."

12

A Lunch With Aliens

"Jeff Wells sir!" shouted Lizzie. "Something is speaking in a foreign language to me through the hull—oh, that's odd. How is it I understand it?"

"Because you're attached to a ship whose computer understands Jamyn," said Norby. "Don't be such an idiot, and tell us what they're saying, since we can't hear it in here."

"I can't help being an idiot. I'm only a Manhattan taxi, at least in my circuits."

"Lizzie, what is whoever it is saying?" asked Jeff.

"I will try to circuit the hull sensors to our loudspeakers," said Mentor First, "since Lizzie is too upset to function adequately. Are most Manhattan taxis like this?"

"Don't answer that, Jeff Wells sir. Please."

Jeff grinned in spite of his anxiety and waited for the sound to come through the loudspeakers. When it did, his heart lifted, for the words were

in that language used by the Others and known
to him as Jamyn.

"Norby? Are you in that strange ship? I felt
mental contact with you, but something is
wrong, for it is not the same. Are you damaged?
Captured?"

"Rembrandt!" Norby clapped his two-way
hands. "Come aboard if you can. We'll unlock
the airlock for you."

When the Other joined them in the control
room, he looked just the age he should be for
Jeff's time, but of course an Other looks the
same until he gets very old.

"We'll explain everything, Rembrandt," said
Jeff. "But first, how long has it been since we
last saw you?"

"Wasn't it a few of your months ago?" asked
Rembrandt. "You'd had your exams and were
on vacation. Is this another vacation?"

"No, it's interterm week and I'm supposed to
be studying for the next batch of exams. Except
that Norby and I got mixed up in some trouble,
and we need your help."

"I'll explain, Jeff," said Norby, reaching for
one of Rembrandt's lower hands. "I'll do it fast,
telepathically."

After a moment, Norby withdrew his hand
and wobbled on his two-way feet. "I couldn't do
it. Somehow I time traveled, and I made Rembrandt sense me over vast distances, but I can't
really communicate telepathically the way I
used to."

"Then I'll do it," said Jeff, "out loud. My contact telepathy isn't good enough to give you a coherent account of what's happened, Rembrandt. In fact, I'm not so sure that any account will be coherent."

Rembrandt and Jeff were eating a solitary meal in the gigantic ship of the Others, with the Jamyn ship plastered airlock to airlock. Norby had decided to stay behind with Lizzie and Mentor First, perhaps because he felt so unhappy over his missing talents.

Humans and the Others are completely different creatures from different parts of the universe, with different histories, yet Jeff felt that he and Rembrandt shared many things in common, especially their biologicality. For one thing, they could breathe the same air and eat similar foods, which is a great help when you want to have a dinner conversation.

"I don't know what will become of Norby if he doesn't get his talents back," said Jeff. "I'm afraid he won't want to stay with me. He may think he'll become just another Terran robot because he can't go all over the universe if he wants to anymore."

"He can still go through time, it seems."

"But he knows that's dangerous."

"Yes, the past must not be changed. Are you afraid Norby will want to stay on Jamya with Mentor First?"

"Yes," said Jeff, his vision suddenly blurry with tears.

"As you know, I am an artist and not skilled

in repairing artificial intelligences, but I have informed my scientists. They are reviewing the problem and will try to help, but I wish you had brought that mysterious gun with you."

"We didn't intend to leave, but if I'd known, I'd probably have left it home anyway. When I was explaining everything to you, I didn't want Mentor First and Norby to know the strange effect the gun had on me when I held it and really thought about it. I didn't want to give it up."

"But you've got no clue as to how it can be used, other than the destructive way that removes robot memory and skills?"

"No. Nothing. You'll have to examine it, Rembrandt, and since you can't possibly show your own ship to Earth, you'll have to leave it here in hyperspace and come with us in our ship. Do you mind?"

Rembrandt rose and paced the polished floor of the rose-colored dining area. A cleaning robot entered, removed the used dishes, and left silently. To Jeff it resembled a walking garbage pail with spidery arms.

When Rembrandt said nothing, Jeff was afraid that he had insulted the much older creature by asking him to come to Earth. "It's not necessary for you to come," Jeff said hurriedly. "We'll go back to Earth, pick up the gun, and reenter hyperspace to meet you again, unless you want to meet us on Jamya or some other planet."

"That is not the problem, Jeff. The problem

is that I want to go to Earth to see your home, to walk on the ground of this Central Park you have described to me. In my entire life, I have walked on the surface of a planet only once, but that was in another universe and I was in a spacesuit. We were trying to save two universes, Jeff. This time I would be going to a planet only because I want to, not because it is necessary."

"You mean you Others have laws saying you can't set foot on planets?"

"We always avoid planets if possible, but we have no laws to regulate our behavior, not anymore. We have gone far past the need for them, perhaps too far. The prohibitions have gradually grown within our own minds. If it were simply a matter of breaking a law, it would be easy. My ancestors, and not-too-distant ones at that, were skilled at breaking laws."

"I remember that you told me you were descended from pirates," said Jeff.

"And after they stopped being pirates, some of them were scavengers, exploring the universe to see what they could pick up that might be of use. It is possible that the gun is one of those things."

"I don't understand. Isn't it something the Others made to send to Jamya on the supply ship that was wrecked?"

"From what you've told me, I don't think so. I have also had our computer search through its historical data banks for anything about a gun like that. There is nothing."

"What does the computer say about the supply ship—the one that is now Mentor First's ship?"

Rembrandt looked uncomfortable. "The data is not there. It's as if someone removed it. I strongly suspect that my own grandfather did it. He was one of the last of the more piratical scavengers, as well as a fine sculptor. He and his crew visited Jamya and left the Mentor robots to be activated so they could bioengineer fierce dragons into the civilized creatures you know. He probably sculpted that bas-relief in Higgins House from memory, for it sounds like a Jamyn dragon. And then he must have sent it in the supply ship as a gift."

"Is there any record of the Others ever making a gun like the one I've described to you?"

"No. Not even way back in our history, when we had an empire that included many solar systems with colonized planets and we were learning to control robots in many ways. We have no device that has the properties Norby experienced, nor those Lizzie learned about from MacGillicuddy. How can such a destructive gun also be used for good?"

"I was hoping you would know."

"We Others of the present day cannot provide that knowledge, Jeff."

"But if you examined the gun, you and your scientists, you might be able to figure out the problem. The gun was probably in a cabinet labeled 'art objects' that your grandfather wanted the Mentor robots on Jamya to have. Does that mean the gun *is* an art object?"

"I don't know." Rembrandt sighed. "I am an artist, so I understand why you want me to look at it. But after the way you reacted to the gun, perhaps some simple robot should take it into your ocean and hide it there. Perhaps it is not wise for any intelligent creature to use it."

"You're an Other. A wiser, older race."

"Not so wise and old that we don't have to take special care not to slide back into being like our ancestors who were less interested in knowledge and creativity than they were in material possessions and power."

"We haven't achieved freedom from those desires," said Jeff. "It wasn't too long ago that humans were almost ready to kill off their own planet in nuclear wars, and after they managed to avoid that, they had to work terribly hard to keep the planet from dying because humans had overpopulated and polluted it."

Rembrandt nodded. "You are a younger race but similar to the way we once were. Now, however, we Others live only in interstellar hyperdrive ships because the various temptations associated with planet living are too dangerous, and by my father's generation we had taken a vow never to interfere in the lives of creatures who live on planets. We keep to this vow even if it sometimes means that we do not help even when help is needed."

"Does that mean you won't help me? You

won't come to Earth to look at the gun, or let me bring it to you?"

Rembrandt leaned forward. "Jeff, my friend, I think you want me to go to your planet, to your very home, and take that gun from the locked drawer so you won't have to touch it again."

Jeff hung his head. "Yes. That's true. I was hoping you would get rid of it for me after you used it to help Norby."

"Are you so certain that it can help him?"

"It's been used twice on Norby—once when he was a Jamyn robot, and then it destroyed his memories of Jamya. The second time was when Merlina used it full strength. It didn't harm Norby's memory banks but it destroyed his alien talents. Yet somehow Moses Mac-Gillicuddy used it in a different way on an old taxi named Lizzie and she became more intelligent."

"Perhaps my scientists will be able to help Norby without using the gun," said Rembrandt, touching a switch. He spoke to somebody using a name as unpronounceable to Jeff as Rembrandt's own real name. Then he asked if the scientists had gone over to the Jamyn ship to examine Norby.

"We have," the voice answered. "He was most cooperative and came back here to be tested by our machines while you and the young human ate dinner. We have sent him back to his own ship now, for we could not diagnose what is wrong, and we cannot repair him."

"I'm sorry, Jeff," said Rembrandt.

"Please, let me bring the gun to you, then."

"Perhaps."

13

Jeff Remembers

Jeff went back to the Jamyn ship carrying some extra food and Rembrandt's gift of five small diamonds, which, suitably sold, could be used to pay the cab company for Lizzie's wreck. Jeff also went back with a heavy heart, for there seemed to be no solution to the problem of restoring Norby's talents, and Rembrandt was not yet willing to examine the gun.

"You shouldn't have told Rembrandt how the gun affected you," said Norby when Jeff told him everything. "The Others seem to be supersensitive about anything that might cause them to be like their ancestors again."

"In Rembrandt's case, he has cause to worry, because his own grandfather was almost a throwback to the more primitive Others. In fact, Rembrandt's grandfather sounds like an alien version of your Mac, exploring space for treasure and anything else he could salvage."

"Why don't we go back in time and meet Rembrandt's grandfather, then? Especially if he's the one who found the gun in the first place. He could tell us how to use it wisely and maybe he could cure me."

"No, Norby. Since Merlina shot you, we've time traveled mostly by accident or guided by your emotive circuits because you wanted to see Mac. I know you successfully brought the ship to our own time period so we could meet Rembrandt, but are you so certain that you have even your time travel ability under control?"

Norby thought for a moment and then blinked. "Maybe I just want to time travel because that's all I can do anymore. And if Rembrandt's grandfather could help..."

"Somehow I doubt it. After all, he may have put the gun in the supply ship being sent to Jamya. I know we thought he did that so the Mentor robots could use it, but maybe his main reason was that he wanted to get rid of it."

"Or, worse yet, the Others were already opposed to interference with planetary life, and he felt guilty about the things he'd already done, like leaving the Mentor robots to change the Jamyn dragons. You and I like Jamya the way it is now, but the Others *did* interfere."

"Then Rembrandt's grandfather sent the gun as an 'art object' so the Mentors would play with it and perhaps destroy themselves! That's terrible! How can we tell Rembrandt that theory?"

"It may not be true, Jeff."

"We can't know for sure. And I think we can't ask Rembrandt's grandfather if he put the gun

in the ship because the very asking may change
the history of the Others. And of Jamya, Mentor
First, you—and me. It's too dangerous, Norby."

"You're right, Jeff. Long ago you and I decided not to time travel unless it was absolutely
necessary, because we've had so many mishaps
doing it. We'd better stick to that, even if it
means I'm just an ordinary robot of no conse-
quence."

Jeff hugged him. "Stop it, Norby. Don't give
up. We'll find a way."

"I'd be better off working as an ordinary robot
on Jamya with my father. As time goes on, he
might find a way to give me new talents and
I'll come back to you, Jeff."

"Will you really come back? By the time you
do, I may be an old man, or dead. Of course, if
you stay with me now, someday I'll die because
I'm only an organic being with a limited lifetime. Then you can go to Jamya to live with
Mentor First, but we'll have been together for
my lifetime, and I want that very much. Please,
Norby, must you go *now?*" Jeff was struggling
to keep from crying, but it was hard.

Norby closed up. His head withdrew into his
body and his hat slammed shut to become the
lid of the barrel. His legs and arms withdrew
until he was only a silvery barrel that had once
borne the label "Norb's Nails."

Jeff waited, conscious of the battle going on
inside Norby's mind. And as he waited, he remembered being back in the taxi called Lizzie,
going home from Higgins House with a silvery

barrel on his lap, with what he thought was a
dead Norby. Lizzie told him then that she'd seen
the gun before, that Mrs. Higgins used it so the
taxi could not inform the police about the robot-
shooting trips.

In his mind, Jeff heard again everything Lizzie said.

"Lizzie!" shouted Jeff. "Can you hear me?"

"No need to shout, Jeff Wells sir. I hear everything that goes on in my taxi. I mean this ship."

"I want you to confirm that I actually
heard..."

"Jeff Wells sir, I did indeed hear Norby say
that he wants to go to Jamya to live. I will be
there, too, because I must go where Mentor
First's ship does. Since I now operate with hyperdrive, I will be happy to ferry you and Norby
back and forth from Earth to Jamya so you can
visit each other."

Norby's head popped up. "You stay out of this,
Lizzie! It's between Jeff and me. You shouldn't
have been listening to our private conversation."

"I don't know how not to, Norby. Mentor First
is in his cabin. Shall I ask him how to turn the
auditory sensors off in the lounge where you
and Jeff are sitting?"

"Now wait, Norby," Jeff began.

"Turn the sensors off!" yelled Norby.

"No!" Jeff picked up Norby and marched to
Mentor First's cabin, knocked on the door, and
waited. When Mentor First opened it, Jeff said,
"Let's all go to the control room. I have some-

thing important to ask Lizzie and you should all be there."

In the control room, Jeff said, "Lizzie, think carefully. When I used your taxi for the first time, going home from Higgins House after Norby was shot, you said that Mrs. Higgins used the gun on you to remove memories of her trips. Then I asked you whether those were the trips to shoot robots, and you said . . ."

"I told you that thanks to Mrs. Higgins shooting me, I couldn't say what happened on the trips."

"No, Lizzie. You didn't say exactly that. Please search your data banks to find the exact words, if you still have them. It's very important."

"My data banks are small, Jeff Wells sir, but after Moses MacGillicuddy changed me, they could retain more information than the usual programming built into Manhattan taxis. I think he must have inserted more microbubble components to enlarge my brain, but ordinary components would not have given me an identity, a feeling of myself as an individual . . ."

"Get on with it, taxi!" said Norby, shoving out his legs and stamping his feet. "Tell Jeff what you actually said."

"I was merely explaining why I have retained the data. Surely that is necessary for adequate understanding—please, Norby, don't pound the control board."

"What did you say that night, Lizzie?" demanded Jeff.

"I said, 'I no longer have access to the memories of those trips. I like Mrs. Higgins's children, but...'"

"That's enough, Lizzie," said Jeff.

"That's *it?*" Norby made a grinding sound. "What use is that?"

Mentor First nodded to Jeff. "I understand. It is the Terran word 'access.' Lizzie, do you mean that the memories are there, inside your mind, and it is only *access* to them that is blocked?"

"Why, yes," said Lizzie. "Didn't everyone realize that? Norby, did you think your talents were actually destroyed, instead of blocked?"

"You blasted idiot of a taxi..."

"Now, Norby, you know I have only a small brain. I am not a genius like you."

"Well," said Norby, clasping one hand on his barrel like a small, silvery Napoleon. "We can't help what we are."

"At any rate," said Jeff soothingly, "we don't have to worry about rebuilding Norby's talents from scratch. All we have to do is remove the block that prevents him from using those talents."

"Much easier," said Mentor First.

"Easier?" said Norby. "And how do you propose to unblock my wonderful talents?"

Nobody had any suggestions. The two robots and the human stared at one another until Lizzie said, "I have a suggestion."

"What?" asked Norby.

"I have already made it. I have broadcast a

recording of everything you and Jeff and Mentor First have said."

"You can't broadcast in hyperspace," said Mentor First.

"You can if two ships are linked," said Lizzie.

Rembrandt came through the airlock and smiled at them. "An interesting development. So Norby's talents are merely blocked, then, not lost. I did not want to encourage you to use the gun or to try it myself, because my grandfather was an old scalawag and I wouldn't trust anything he found and kept secretly. Furthermore, I feared that next time the gun might destroy all of Norby's mind. But now that we know the gun does not actually destroy . . ."

"If you can trust a pea brain like Lizzie's," snapped Norby.

"I am ready to go with you to Earth," said Rembrandt. "And I will examine that gun. But it is you, Jeff, who must use it. Norby is your robot."

"Ready to emerge from hyperspace?" asked Lizzie. "I rather like giving orders to the stupid computer on this ship."

"Go ahead, Lizzie," said Mentor First. "Take us to the exact coordinates of Jeff's rooftop. The computer has them."

"Sure," said Lizzie, "but *I* won't deposit this hulk on the rooftop until I see there's no taxi there!"

14

The Work of Art

"Worried? Why shouldn't I be worried? There I was, immersed in the most difficult plot a novelist has ever attempted, to say nothing of the subtly graphic description of a seething love affair that kept getting out of hand..."

Fargo paused for breath and scowled at his brother. "Since I couldn't go up to the roof to find out why you never came back from a talk with Lizzie, I had to call for help."

"I was only gone from breakfast until tea-time," said Jeff calmly, taking a careful swallow because the decaffeinated Earl Grey tea was hot. "I'd have let you know except that, as I carefully explained, we were preoccupied."

It was too late to try to conceal anything from Hedy Higgins and Leo Jones, who sat side by side on the couch and had obviously been told everything by a distraught Fargo.

Hedy smiled at Rembrandt. "You Others are

so different, and yet we humans feel at home with you."

"There is a comradeship of intelligence, Miss Higgins," said Rembrandt, speaking the Terran Basic he had speed-learned perfectly, albeit with a strong Manhattan accent, from Lizzie via the computer in the Jamyn ship.

"I admit," Rembrandt continued, "that this comradeship is easier and quicker if the different species are both bilaterally symmetrical, walk on legs, and breathe the same atmosphere." He laughed, and it sounded quite human. "I am amazed at the beauty of your Earth and the diversity of cultures within your civilization."

"If you liked that videocube we just showed you, wait 'til you hear some of our music," said Leo. "I've just found out that Hedy sings in a chorus and I'm going to join."

"Leo has a lovely baritone," said Hedy. They smiled and squeezed each other's hands. It was noticeable that no matter what the subject, Leo and Hedy eventually started talking about their blooming relationship.

Jeff was impatient with the middle-aged lovers because he had Norby's plight on his mind, as well as the prospect of Norby going to live on Jamya if he couldn't be cured.

"Hedy, do you know where your mother found the gun she used to shoot Norby?"

"I asked her the other day. She said it was in the tube. I asked her what tube, and she said, 'At the back of me.' She refused to say any more.

Most of the time she won't talk at all. Horace and I are very worried about her. We had the doctor over, and he says she's not ill, just depressed. But medicines made her feel sick and she refused to take them."

"Tube," said Norby. "The shape of a pipe. That might be what was held by the clamps in the ship's cabinet. Mac took the tube away with him and either found the gun in it or put the gun there later."

"Hedy," said Jeff, "will you take me to your mother? I must talk to her. How else can we find out what the tube was? Maybe she still has it somewhere and the directions are still in it. I'd rather try to find the directions before I experiment with the gun."

"I want to go with you, Jeff," said Rembrandt. "I must see the dragon sculpture that my grandfather probably made, and I want to walk through Central Park in the snow."

Everyone began to talk at once, Fargo heatedly exclaiming that Rembrandt had to be kept hidden; Leo saying he couldn't provide security for such a distinguished visitor; Norby saying that since he didn't dare go inside Higgins House again for fear of upsetting Merlina even more, Rembrandt should stay behind with him; Jeff saying that the Other had no boots anyway and the park was cold and wet.

Hedy interrupted them. "Rembrandt's feet— I think they are feet—are small enough to fit into Fargo's overshoes. I will go ahead in a taxi to prepare my family for visitors. I will explain

that Jeff's friend is an actor starring in a new
film about haunted houses and that he wants
to see Higgins House for inspiration. Horace
loves videocube movies about haunted houses,
and Mother . . . well, Mother is the other dragon
in the house that you must see."

"How can Rembrandt masquerade as an actor when he has four arms and three eyes?"
Fargo asked.

"Where's your adventurous spirit, Fargo?"
asked Hedy, the light of battle in her eyes. Jeff
was reminded of Hedy as he'd first met her—a
lady who pummeled villains with her umbrella.

"Rembrandt can wear the ski mask that hid
Mentor First's upper eye," said Jeff. "Then he'll
just look like a slightly odd hairless person,
especially if he wears your cape, Fargo. Everyone will assume he *is* an actor. You know how
many movies are made here in Manhattan."

"I don't think you should go without me," said
Norby.

"You must stay home, Norby. Mentor First,
see that he does, please."

"Yes, Jeff." Mentor First hadn't said much at
all. He seemed to be in awe of Rembrandt because he was the grandson of the Other who
had made Mentor First.

"Should I take the gun with me?" asked Jeff.
"The sight of it might jog Merlina's memory so
we can find the directions quicker."

Nobody ventured a reply until Fargo
shrugged. "Up to you and Rembrandt. I noticed
he hasn't asked to see it yet."

"I told you how the gun made me feel," said Jeff. "It's dangerous."

"You told all of us at great length," said Fargo, "but I'm not impressed. You have the most marvelous robot in the universe..."

"I used to be," said Norby.

"... and you've never exploited him for power or treated him as a mere possession. Why should you lose control of your goodness and become a villain?"

"Gee..."

"Unless you want to, that is."

"Fargo! I don't..." Jeff paused. "Why does that remind me of something? Something about the gun." He ran into his room, unlocked the desk drawer, and returned with the gun held carefully so he was not touching the trigger depression.

Rembrandt bent over Jeff's outstretched hand. "That device is completely alien."

"It's certainly not made on Earth, or in any of the extraterrestrial parts of our Solar Federation," said Leo.

"I think Rembrandt means that the gun was not made by the Others either," said Norby. "Jeff, how do you react to the gun this time?"

Jeff stood very still. "Wait. Everybody keep quiet for a moment." He closed his eyes and concentrated on the gun.

It was like holding something of great power, yet the power was indefinite... no, more than that. Suddenly Jeff knew that the power depended on the person holding the gun. He could control the strength, the direction, and, yes, the action of the gun, if he knew how.

The odd thing was that Jeff had experienced similar feelings before in his life, especially when he was quite young; but now he couldn't remember what had been going on at the time he'd felt that way.

"Are you all right, Jeff?" asked Norby.

"I wish I could remember. Power . . . such satisfaction . . . such happiness . . ."

"Jeff!" Leo was at his side, shaking him.

Jeff opened his eyes. "I'm all right. I think."

"Maybe you'd better lock that blasted thing up again," said Fargo. "You look as if you'd found a magic ring of the ancient gods."

"Perhaps I have," said Jeff. "Or I will as soon as I figure out what the feeling means."

"You're beginning to worry me," said Rembrandt. "Perhaps this expedition is not a good idea."

Hedy stood up and said, "Overcoats, capes, and boots. Jeff and Rembrandt. Norby needs help. My mother damaged him and if we can get information from her that will help Norby, we must try. Now that I know from the doctor that she is in no danger of dying, I am willing to be tougher on her."

"But how will Horace react to Rembrandt?" asked Leo.

"My good but childlike brother will be delighted to show off the dragon over the mantel while I take Jeff upstairs to talk to my poor mother."

• • •

It was a long walk, for Jeff found that he had to show Rembrandt all his favorite places on the way through the park, and by the time they arrived at Higgins House, its peaked roof was lit by the blaze of the sunset in the west.

"That is a sunset," said Rembrandt, as if savoring the Terran word. "It needs a more beautiful word."

"The sun doesn't always set in beauty. Sometimes it's raining or snowing, especially in Manhattan in winter."

"The closure of daylight on a planet, followed by the dark of night, is always beautiful, like life itself."

"Too short," mourned Jeff, realizing that the happy young Mac he'd talked to had been dead for years, and that Mac's beautiful daughter was an unhappy old woman who had tried to destroy the robot she thought of as a rival.

"You humans live for a short time compared to us, yet all biological lives are ultimately brief in a huge universe."

"Do you think that even the briefest life can contribute something to the development of the universe?"

"Ah, Jeff Wells. That is why I am an artist."

The door opened and Horace grinned at them. "Welcome to Higgins House, sir. If you can't get inspiration for your movie here, you can't get it anywhere. If you'll just step to the doorway, I will demonstrate our gargoyle's talents."

Jeff hastily pulled Rembrandt onto the doorsill as Horace tugged at a rope. Instantly, a stream of purple water shot down to make a dark splotch on the snow.

"I colored the water," said Horace proudly.

Jeff took Rembrandt outside again and pointed to the gargoyle, a wicked-looking object in the gathering dusk. He whispered in Jamyn, "Do you think your grandfather made that, too?"

"No," said Rembrandt. "It's undoubtedly one of Moses MacGillicuddy's sculptures, and jokes."

They went inside the hall and Rembrandt stopped before the fireplace mantel. "Grandfather, undoubtedly. It looks as if he had fun with that one, too."

"You mean, it's a device . . ."

"No. Just a sculpture that he enjoyed doing. But there is something else here that is—different. Not Grandfather's. Not from the Others at all. Something like the gun—alien."

"Please," begged Horace. "I know that you movie people come from all over the solar system, but I wish you wouldn't speak another language. This is my only chance to listen . . ."

"Horace," said Jeff, "this is a very private meeting. It's a secret movie. You must not tell anyone who we are or what we're saying."

"I won't. Besides, I don't talk to anyone but you folks and Hedy and Mother. Who would I tell?"

"Come up, Jeff," called Hedy from the landing. She had just turned on the lights and the portrait of Merlina Mynn gazed down on them.

"Strange as the human face and form is to an Other," said Rembrandt, "I know that that is a particularly lovely woman. I wonder why the portrait seems alien to me, although the woman is clearly human."

"Alien!" Jeff took the gun from his pocket. "Do you mean alien like this gun? Something not even the Others made?"

"Yes, Jeff. I think we should go home. That portrait is perhaps as dangerous as the gun."

Jeff ran to the landing and looked closely at the portrait, but Rembrandt stayed down in the hall with Horace.

"From here the surface seems smooth, as if the portrait's been covered by glass or plasti-film," said Jeff. "I don't know what you mean by 'alien,' Rembrandt."

"It can't be alien," said Hedy. "That's how my mother looked when she was an actress, before Grandfather died. She said she found it rolled up among the gear he'd brought from his ship. That's why she assumed he'd taken it with him on his salvage trips."

"Rolled up?" said Jeff. "To form a tube?"

"Oh, Jeff! How stupid of me! You asked where Mother found the gun and I told you she said 'in the tube.' Perhaps she meant the rolled-up painting."

"You fools," said the husky voice of Merlina Mynn. She came slowly down the stairs to the landing. "The painting was rolled up in a metal tube for safekeeping on all those voyages my

father took. How else would he have kept it in
his cabin, away from the prying eyes of that
robot of his? He wanted the portrait to himself."

"Was this gun inside the rolled-up painting
in the metal tube?" asked Jeff, showing it to
Merlina.

"Yes," she said. "They came together." Her
white hair was loose around her face, and she
looked like a witch.

"And where is the tube now?" asked Jeff.

Merlina's shoulders lifted slightly. Her exotic
eyes looked dead in her pale face. "Where it's
always been, behind my portrait. When I
brought the painting home from the framers I
realized that it wouldn't hang right because the
molding at the top of the wall sticks out so
much. I fastened the tube to the bottom of the
frame to balance things. Take the portrait
down, Hedy. I want to get rid of it."

"But, Mother, I want it," said Horace.

"Perhaps we should give it away," said Hedy,
"if that will make Mother feel better. And don't
worry, Horace. I took a photograph of the portrait yesterday, so you can have that."

"But I love the portrait!"

"Yes, Horace," said Merlina. "Everyone loves
that portrait more than they love me. My father
preferred it. Hedy, give the portrait away! Give
it to that actor down there. He can use it as
part of the scenery in his movie. Is it a horror
movie, mister actor?"

"I don't know yet," said Rembrandt.

Hedy lifted the portrait down and turned it

around. Fixed to the bottom of the frame was a hollow metal cylinder the right size to contain the rolled-up portrait. Hedy looked into the tube. "It's empty. And there's nothing written on it."

"Mrs. Higgins..." Jeff began.

"I am Merlina Mynn."

"Miss Mynn, do you remember what else was in the tube besides the portrait and the gun? Was there a piece of paper, or anything with writing of any sort on it?"

"Oh, yes," said Merlina. "I threw it away."

Jeff gritted his teeth. "Do you remember what it said? Or was it in a language you couldn't read?"

"Of course I could read it, young man. It was a page torn from one of my father's notebooks. He'd scribbled on it some silly words."

"Mother, you shouldn't have thrown them out!" said Hedy.

"Why? I'm an actress. I can memorize anything. I remember. The words were, 'Thoughts make the difference.'"

"That's all?" Jeff asked.

"Yes. Unlike myself, Father was becoming senile as he aged. I suppose I should forgive him for treasuring a portrait instead of me, but I can't. Give the portrait to the actor."

Rembrandt stepped closer, looking up at Merlina Mynn. She stared down at him and shuddered.

"Are you made up to look that way, or have you just put on that insufferable expression of compassion? Stop looking as if you wanted to forgive me my sins."

"Miss Mynn, only you can forgive yourself," said Rembrandt. "Stop living with hate."

"I like hate! It keeps me warm! It makes me feel alive!"

"No," said Rembrandt. "It is killing you and blighting the lives of those you love."

"I love no one."

"That is not true," said Rembrandt, in a voice like thunder. "Think, Miss Mynn. Think of those you have loved who are dead and those who are still alive."

"Think of us, Mother," said Hedy. "Horace and I love you even if you hate..."

"No! Thoughts make a difference, and I am imprisoned in mine. I am Merlina Mynn...the great...the magical..." She broke off and sobbed. When Hedy tried to put an arm around her, Merlina shook it off and lunged at Jeff, snatching the gun from his hand.

"Miss Mynn, don't..."

"I'm going to shoot! I hate you—die!" She pointed the gun and pushed her thumb hard into the trigger groove.

15

The Legacy

Merlina Mynn was pointing the alien gun at the portrait of herself. Jeff wrested the gun out out of her grip, but it was too late. The image had disappeared.

"Hah!" said Merlina. "I feel better already. That portrait has tortured me since I found it. Go away, you strangers. I am free of the past now. Free to die in peace."

"Mother!" yelled Horace. "Don't die! I need you! When Hedy marries the mayor and goes to live in Gracie Mansion, I'll be all alone! Please don't leave me."

"That's what I'll have left?" asked Merlina. "A drafty old house to live in with an addled son who will no doubt put a photo of my portrait in his ridiculous workshop that you children thought you could hide from me?"

Horace burst into tears and ran into a side room off the main hall.

"Mother, you're unkind," said Hedy. "In fact,

you're a witch of an old woman. Do you want
me to hate you as much as you hate yourself?
Well, then, go ahead and die. Horace will come
with me to Gracie Mansion."

Merlina sniffed and started back up the staircase.

"Miss Mynn!" said Rembrandt.

"Well? Are you angry because you can't have
the portrait I told Hedy to give you?"

"I wish to have what is left."

Merlina tossed her hair back, her chin high.
For an instant she looked like a magnificent
young woman made up to resemble Medea after
the killing. "You can't have it. Hedy, hang the
frame back in place. Every time I go downstairs
I will remember that I have destroyed the past."

As Hedy rehung the frame, enclosing a blank
surface, Jeff mounted the stairs toward Merlina. He still held the gun. She turned to con-
front him.

"What are you going to do, young man,
threaten me with that gun? It doesn't work on
people. I tried years ago. There's no effect."

"There's an effect on the people who hold the
gun," said Jeff. "I think your father was right.
Thoughts make a difference—to this gun. It re-
sponds to the thoughts and emotions of the person holding it."

"No," said Merlina, her face much paler. "I
won't believe that. Tell me it isn't so."

Jeff tried to think of a way to tell Merlina
without hurting her too much. He had lost his
anger, and he pitied her.

"When you pointed the gun at your own portrait, what did you feel?"

"That I wanted to get rid of it."

"Mother," said Hedy, "your emotions were stronger than that. You said that you hated it. That you wanted it to die."

"Did you think that if you shot the portrait, you yourself would die, Mrs. Higgins?" asked Jeff.

"Yes," she whispered. "That's what I really want. I am a bad person, just as the little robot said. I wanted to die, but I didn't. Only the portrait died—that young and beautiful, kind and noble woman I never became."

The hall was silent while they looked at her, and Jeff saw that her hatred was gone.

The doorbell rang and Horace reappeared in the hall. "I called up the Wellses' apartment and spoke to Jeff's brother. I thought we needed help. The robots are here."

"Robots!" said Merlina, putting her hand to her lips.

"You didn't kill your father's robot," said Jeff, "but you damaged him."

Horace opened the door and three beings walked in. One of them was human and came immediately to Hedy.

"Hedy, m'love," said Leo. "I couldn't let the robots go alone, when I could explain to the cops that I'm the mayor and they are part of a project I'm working on. In fact, we were stopped twice, once crossing Fifth Avenue, and the other time just outside Higgins House. I must compliment my daughter on the alertness of the police force."

"Besides, he can't stand being away from Hedy for very long," said Norby, walking up to Jeff on the landing. "Hello, Mrs. Higgins. I mean Miss Mynn. Can I help you?"

"You want to help me after what I did to you?"

"Yes, because I know how much Mac loved you."

"You think he loved me because you saw that portrait in his ship?"

"No, ma'am. I never saw the portrait. He didn't like anyone to go into his cabin. But I know. Don't ask how."

"If only I could believe you!"

"Miss Mynn," said Jeff, "you used the gun on the portrait and it vanished. I think that an unknown artist from long ago and very far away invented the gun as a tool for artists, like a paintbrush. When I hold the gun I feel just the way I did when I was a little kid and I was given a set of paints and an easel to play with. I held the brush and felt so powerful, thinking about what I could create. Naturally, the feeling went away quickly because I wasn't much good as an artist—but Moses MacGillicuddy was."

"Then my father created the portrait himself?"

"From the way he thought of you," said Jeff. "Or the way he wanted you to be."

"Then that was my legacy," said Merlina.

"The portrait itself. On his deathbed he tried to tell me how valuable it was. But he also said the word 'truth.' The portrait was a lie, for I was not like that."

"But he knew you could be," said Jeff. "Truth is also the potential in each of us."

"It is never too late, Mother," said Hedy.

"Late?" Merlina Mynn drew herself upright, her eyes bright. "I am my father's daughter. Of course it's not too late. I am going to go on living. I am going to be a nice person, good and kind and..."

"Don't overdo it, Mother," said Hedy.

Merlina laughed. She looked radiant. "Perhaps I'll never be exactly what my father wanted me to be, but I'm going to try, now that I know he cared." Then her face drooped back into tragedy. "If I hadn't destroyed the portrait!"

"I'll have the photograph blown up," said Hedy. "You and Horace can both have copies."

"I miss my father!" said Merlina, old again.

"Miss Mynn," said Norby, "now that I undersand what the two devices are—a sort of canvas and a sort of paintbrush—I want to give you something. Jeff, please let me have the thing we've been calling a gun."

Jeff handed the gun to Norby, who pointed it at the blank surface where the portrait of Merlina had been.

"Be careful, Norby," said Rembrandt. "You are already damaged. Be sure the gun does not hurt you any more."

Norby held the gun steadily pointed in the right direction and shut all four of his eyes. His oddly jointed thumb pressed into the recessed switch.

At first, nothing happened, and then there was a gradual clouding of the alien surface. Soon it seemed to be boiling with writhing colors and shapes.

"What are you doing?" cried Merlina. "Are you showing me the hatred that has obsessed me for too many years?"

"No, ma'am," said Norby. "I'm sorting out my memories."

"Look!" said Horace. "That's Grandfather!"

The friendly, piratical, and neatly framed face of Moses MacGillicuddy looked down on the assembled group. He was not as young as when Jeff had encountered him, but he was not a feeble old man either.

"That's a remarkable portrait, Norby," said Leo. "Did you do it with the gun?"

"With my mind," said Norby. "With my love for Mac. The gun just channels and augments the energy of my cognitive and emotive circuits, and the surface of that material creates the image that I want."

Merlina walked down to the landing and touched her father's image. "I am proud to be his daughter. I will treasure this portrait, little Norby. Thank you."

16

The Problem Remains

"All's well that ends well?" asked Fargo, polishing off his dessert of a red Macintosh apple. "Higgins House is now full of sweetness and light?"

"We haven't ended Norby's problem," said Jeff. "His special talents are still blocked. I spent an hour trying with the gun after we got home, but nothing happened."

"Have an apple, Jeff," said Fargo. "Don't worry so much."

Mentor First and Norby had gone to the roof to keep Lizzie company while the biologicals ate dinner. Jeff was glad that Rembrandt had been able to eat the only thing the kitchen computer seemed up to producing that night—soy fritters. He was also glad that Hedy and Leo were eating with Merlina and Horace, planning a wedding and improvements to Higgins House.

"I can't understand why the gun—I still

think of it as that—didn't work when I thought very hard about Norby's blocked talents as I pressed the trigger."

"Jeff!" yelled Fargo. "The human mind does not function adequately when preoccupied with anxious ruminations. Stop thinking and try to relax."

"Perhaps," said Rembrandt calmly, "the gun has a limited amount of energy that has been used up. I am sorry that neither Mentor First nor I have been able to sense what the mechanism is or how it works. I suppose that if we could, it wouldn't help, since it is utterly alien to both humans and Others."

"Then what are we going to do?" cried Jeff.

"I think you must accept Norby the way he is."

"He won't accept himself," said Jeff. "He'll go with Mentor First, hoping and hoping that some day the Jamyn robots will be able to repair him."

"Perhaps they will," said Rembrandt gently.

"I don't want to give up so easily, Rembrandt. I'm only a human being, and I'm young, but I'm going to keep trying."

"You humans are stubborn and courageous. I admire you." Rembrandt stroked the green fur of Oola, who was curled up in his lap and purring loudly.

"You're an artist," said Jeff, trying to think clearly in spite of his anguish. "You're also a supercivilized being, so you were able to let

Merlina Mynn keep the alien thing that acts as a canvas."

"Thanks to Norby," said Rembrandt, "the alien surface is now a work of art that can be appreciated and loved by human beings. Without the gun, the portrait of MacGillicuddy will remain just as it is and will harm no one, so I think it is safe to leave the alien surface here on Earth."

"That doesn't make sense," said Fargo through the apple. "How can there be potential harm in the picture-making surface when the gun isn't around?"

"The picture that forms on that surface shows inner truth to those who see it. Merlina could not stand seeing the truth of her own potential that she thwarted. But Norby's love for MacGillicuddy has produced a portrait that makes everyone feel better just to look at it."

"That's true," said Jeff. "But is the gun dangerous even when it's just used as a paintbrush, so to speak?"

The eye in Rembrandt's forehead closed momentarily and it was a minute before he spoke. "I am guessing, but I think it is possible that my grandfather found the alien gun-brush and the alien surface that acts as a canvas. He was an artist and a rascal, so he didn't tell anyone and kept them for himself, but perhaps during his experiments he discovered two dangerous aspects to the gun."

"Two?" asked Fargo. "It seems to me that the

only danger is if the gun is used to block robot abilities."

"There is a danger to the biological being who holds the gun," said Rembrandt. "It is not the sense of power that Jeff felt, for any artist experiences that when he holds the tools he is skilled at using. I think my grandfather got rid of the gun because it increases the capacity of its user to create from emotion."

"I understand," said Jeff. "If the emotion is not a good one, the work of art may be unpleasant."

"Or much worse," said Rembrandt. "An artist who owned that gun would have to take it out only after deep meditation and mental discipline put him in a state fit to use it."

"That sends chills over me," said Jeff. "Maybe I should be glad the energy of the gun has run out. I might have damaged Norby, trying it on him when I'm so anxious."

"Then go to sleep, Jeff," said Fargo brusquely. "In the morning we're going to try to charge up that blasted gun so we can help Norby."

"But Rembrandt just explained how dangerous . . ."

"Shut up and go to bed, young one. Rembrandt, I happen to have a videocube of the paintings by your human namesake. Would you care to see it?"

"Very much so, if you take back your pet. She is now deeply asleep, apparently dreaming of catching small animals. She keeps digging her claws into my lower extremities."

Jeff went to bed, certain that he would not sleep. Then he heard a metallic singing from the roof. Lizzie and Mentor First were harmonizing on a rather ribald song she had undoubtedly taught him.

Finally he heard another voice join in, slightly off-key. That could only be Norby.

He's happy with them, thought Jeff. They'll all go to Jamya to live, without me.

Jeff found himself feeling angry and abandoned, just the way Merlina Mynn had felt, only not as bad.

"I won't be like that," he whispered. "I'll let Norby go if that's what's best for him."

After that it was easier to fall asleep.

The next morning after breakfast Rembrandt and Jeff went up to the ship on the roof. Fargo insisted on going too, so Mentor First carried him, boots and all. They sat in the control room of the Jamyn ship and discussed the problem.

"There's no way to plug this thing in," said Jeff, looking at the gun-brush as it lay on the control board. "How can we recharge it, if that's what has to be done?"

Mentor First picked it up. "There is a tiny hole in the closed end. Perhaps a wire stuck in there could convey electricity to whatever's inside."

"But what kind of electricity?" asked Norby.

"Direct current or alternating current? And what voltage?"

"We can't know," said Rembrandt. "We'll have to experiment to find out, taking the risk that instead of charging the gun we'll damage it irreparably."

"MacGillicuddy didn't." Jeff gulped as everyone stared at him as if he'd gone crazy. "I mean, Mac must have used the gun quite a bit—on Norby, and maybe on other robots we don't know about, and on Lizzie to improve her brain. He also created the portrait of his daughter, perhaps after many trials."

"In other words," said Fargo, "Mac must have depleted the gun's energy and learned to recharge it."

"The gun may have had a great deal of energy to begin with," said Mentor First. "This may be the first time it has run down."

"But maybe not," said Jeff. "Let's take the chance that Mac did recharge it, and figure out what he had to do."

"All Terran ships use alternating current now," said Fargo. "And they did when Mac was running around the solar system with the gun and the picture-surface in his ship."

"Even if he recharged the gun at Higgins House, that's on alternating current, too," said Jeff. "What does this ship use, Mentor First?"

"Alternating current, but different from your apartment."

"I can regulate the amount sent to the gun," said Lizzie, "but I can't change the current to direct. Not until I've had more time to adjust..."

"You couldn't then, either," said Mentor First. "The electricity from our motors is standardized and unchangeable."

Everyone sank into gloom at that, until Jeff said, "We'll have to try it anyway. Let's hook it up."

Mentor First attached a wire to one of Lizzie's terminals and stuck the other end into the gun. "Go ahead, Lizzie."

"Nothing's happening," said Lizzie. "The juice isn't being used at all. Try the apartment sockets."

They trouped down to the apartment and tried there, but the gun still didn't work, even when Jeff tried it out on the housekeeping robot.

They went back to the Jamyn ship to see if Lizzie had any other ideas.

"No. I do wish Mac were here, because he'd know. He was always playing with electrical things, buying equipment for a set of toy trains Horace had when he was a little boy."

Mentor First opened a compartment in his middle and took out the transistors and the transformer that Horace had given him. "Equipment like this?"

"Yes," said Lizzie. "I was always on call to take Mac on errands to the stores. He loved his grandchildren, especially Horace, who was much older than Hedy."

Fargo took the old transformer and laughed.

"Wouldn't it be funny if this gadget, so simple a kid can make one, helped change the current to fit the gun?"

"Let's try it," said Jeff.

Mentor First and Fargo fussed with the wires and the hookup until Lizzie said, "Okay, boys. I'm going to try."

A full five minutes passed, and Jeff could stand the suspense no longer. "What's happening, Lizzie? Is there any hope of recharging the gun?"

"Oh, it's recharging. Simple as pie, Jeff Wells sir. There, it's done. Try it now."

Jeff held the gun and was instantly frozen with fear. He felt as if he were holding a genuine loaded gun, not an artist's device for channeling the energy of thoughts and emotions into the creation of something beautiful or helpful.

"I can't. I'm afraid."

Rembrandt touched Jeff's shoulder. "You and Norby should be alone. We'll stay here with Lizzie and you two go down to the apartment."

In the Wellses' living room, Norby sat on the couch while Oola sat on the floor next to Jeff's chair, burping slightly as she digested her daily meal of fresh vegetables.

"Go ahead, Jeff. I trust you," said Norby.

"I don't trust myself. I feel inadequate."

"You are my owner and my friend. I intend to stay with you even if you don't succeed in unblocking my talents."

"You will, Norby? Gosh, that's wonderful." Jeff closed his eyes and thought about Norby—

a funny-looking barrel of a robot but a wondrous companion, who could take his owner through hyperspace to faraway parts of the universe, who could join minds to share thoughts...

Holding the gun, lost in a sense of creative power, Jeff felt himself become one with Norby, with his image of Norby. He smiled, opened his eyes, and pressed the trigger.

17

Up From Earth

"Goodbye, Rembrandt," said Jeff. "I'm glad I persuaded you to take the gun. You're the best artist I know, and if anyone can use it, you can."

"First, my people have to invent the picture-surface found by MacGillicuddy. I think that will be easier than trying to invent the gun. Thanks to you and Norby, I am no longer afraid, for I have seen that even a dangerous tool can be used properly, if it is handled with love."

"I hope you will visit Earth again and stay longer. There's so much that Norby and I want to show you."

"I'll return, perhaps with a new painting to show *you*."

Jeff went back to the Jamyn ship through the airlock and heard Lizzie say, "Okay, Jeff Wells sir, shall we go on to Jamya to drop off Mentor First?"

"And you, Lizzie. You're part of his ship, remember?"

"That's what I've been talking to Norby about. I really want to be a taxi again. All this traveling about in space and hyperspace makes me wish I were down to Earth in dear old Manhattan. And I miss the Higgins family."

"I think we can do something about that," said Jeff.

It was quiet in the Space Academy room. Jeff was studying for his last exam at one computer terminal, and Norby was whizzing over the keyboard of another.

Norby chuckled. "This is going to be great. *My* novel will be full of humor and poignant interpersonal relationships. Let Fargo try to beat *me* as a writer."

"I'm relieved that you've decided not to write a biography of MacGillicuddy," said Jeff.

"It would no doubt be a best seller and ruin our privacy, especially mine." Norby's back eyes blinked at his owner. "You know, staying down to Earth is all very well, but what I like best is being with you here in Space Academy."

"I like Space Academy, too," said Jeff. "I'm just another cadet, you're my teaching robot, and I can study in peace and quiet..."

The equations on Jeff's computer screen blanked out and were replaced by the face of Admiral Boris Yobo, who was frowning more fiercely than usual.

"Cadets are not allowed to make personal hy-com calls unless it is an emergency. Furthermore, cadets are not allowed to charge *any* hycom calls to *my* personal account!"

"But I didn't . . ."

"Admiral," said Norby, "I'm a little short of funds, so I didn't think you'd mind if we spoke to the invalid."

"Fargo's had another accident?"

"No, he's almost recovered from the last one."

"Then why . . ." The admiral's head turned. "What's that? Oh, all right. I accept charges. Norby, your call's come through. Here's Fargo. Don't let it happen again, or I'll take away your computer terminal before you finish whatever it is you think you're writing on it."

The admiral's face disappeared and Fargo grinned at them. "I assume you want news, so here's your friendly Terran reporter with the latest. The wedding plans are going full blast. You'll carry the groom's top hat, Norby. Merlina is having a new wardrobe made, which she can afford because she's the star of a new soap opera. She has also become rich enough to buy Lizzie's new taxi, so you can use the rest of Rembrandt's diamonds for your education, Jeff. Now let's see, have I forgotten anything? Oh, yes, my boots came off and my ankles are perfect, as handsome as ever, according to my beautiful Albany."

"But what about Mac's memorial?" shouted Norby. "I told you to talk Leo Jones into it!"

"My future father-in-law says that Central Park will soon boast a statue of his grandfather-in-law-to-be."

"It's about time," said Norby.

"And the statue will be carrying a silver barrel with a lid on it. This is bound to cause confusion among spectators . . ."

"Now *that's* a fitting memorial for Mac!" Norby paused. "But what can we do to keep pigeons off the statue of *me?*"